"There's something else," Dean said, carefully.

His tone put her further on edge.

She raised her brows, unable to voice the question. What else had gone wrong now?

"Given the events of the day I think it would be wise for you and Blakely to leave the apartment. At least until the danger stops coming every time we stand still long enough to take a deep breath."

Nicole nodded. "Are you asking me to move to the ranch?"

"No." He cleared his throat. "I thought you could stay with me."

Nicole's mouth opened, then shut without comment.

"I'd sleep on the couch. I'm not suggesting anything—" his cheeks darkened slightly, the blush plainly visible "—that would make you uncomfortable."

"I know," she said. "I know you."

Their gazes locked. Her heart rate climbed for new reasons as she fell deeper into the depths of his baby blues.

CLOSING IN ON CLUES

JULIE ANNE LINDSEY

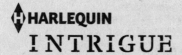

For my incredible friend Nicole Homes.

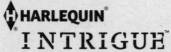

Recycling programs
for this product may
not exist in your area.

ISBN-13: 978-1-335-59124-1

Closing In On Clues

Copyright © 2023 by Julie Anne Lindsey

For questions and comments about the quality of this book,
please contact us at CustomerService@Harlequin.com.

Harlequin Enterprises ULC
22 Adelaide St. West, 41st Floor
Toronto, Ontario M5H 4E3, Canada
www.Harlequin.com

Printed in U.S.A.

Julie Anne Lindsey is an obsessive reader who was once torn between the love of her two favorite genres: toe-curling romance and chew-your-nails suspense. Now she gets to write both for Harlequin Intrigue. When she's not creating new worlds, Julie can be found carpooling her three kids around northeastern Ohio and plotting with her shamelessly enabling friends. Winner of the Daphne du Maurier Award for Excellence in Mystery/Suspense, Julie is a member of International Thriller Writers, Romance Writers of America and Sisters in Crime. Learn more about Julie and her books at julieannelindsey.com.

Books by Julie Anne Lindsey

Harlequin Intrigue

Beaumont Brothers Justice

Closing In On Clues

Heartland Heroes

SVU Surveillance
Protecting His Witness
Kentucky Crime Ring
Stay Hidden
Accidental Witness
To Catch a Killer

Visit the Author Profile page at Harlequin.com.

CAST OF CHARACTERS

Nicole Homes—A thirty-one-year-old elementary school teacher whose younger sister went missing following a catering job at a private party. Nicole will stop at nothing to protect her niece and recover her sister.

Dean Beaumont—A thirty-four-year-old private investigator determined to protect Nicole and her niece while bringing Nicole's missing sister home safely. Dean enlists the help of his family—comprised of local law enforcement, investigators and former military—to get the job done.

Cari Homes—A new mother and current missing person with a troubled past. Cari vanished from a catering job in an elite Marshal's Bluff, North Carolina, neighborhood.

Blakely Homes—Five-month-old daughter of Cari, currently in her aunt Nicole's care.

Mr. and Mrs. Beaumont—Beaumont family patriarch and matriarch, owners of a restorative ranch, working hard to improve lives in their small coastal community.

Detective Finn Beaumont—Working with his brothers and police department to bring Nicole's sister home safely.

Mr. Tippin—Luxury car dealership manager and owner of the home where Cari was last seen.

Chapter One

Nicole Homes checked the clock for the tenth time in half as many minutes, a routine she'd perfected hours before, when her younger sister, Cari, went from being inconsiderably late to unfathomably so. There'd been a time in Cari's teen years when staying out all night without calling meant she'd fallen back into bad habits and unhealthy patterns, but she'd been clean for thirty-five months. And since the birth of her daughter, Blakely, in the spring, Cari tended to come home early more often than not.

So where was she now?

"Of course I've tried calling," Nicole explained to a painfully calm officer on the other end of the line. "I get voice mail every time."

She paced the living room carpet with impatient steps and a biting urge to scream. If it hadn't been for her sweet niece, playing happily in the nearby playpen, she might have.

"Something's happened to my sister," she repeated. "I know it."

And whatever it is, it's bad, she thought, and her breaths grew increasingly shallow.

"I understand your concern, ma'am," the officer replied. "I do. But without any evidence of foul play, your sister is just considered late at this point. You said she worked last night."

"Only until eleven."

"All right. Maybe she got caught up. Maybe the party where she worked went on longer than expected, or she went out with friends afterward and fell asleep."

"Okay," Nicole conceded. "Then where is she now? It's nearly lunchtime."

The officer inhaled audibly, then released the breath on a slow exhale. "It's barely ten a.m. She could still be sleeping if she had a late night. Maybe she had car trouble. Maybe her phone is dead, because she didn't take a charger to work with her. Any number of very common, non-perilous things could've happened, and nine times out of ten, that's all it is. Hang tight until this evening, and if she's still not home after twenty-four hours…"

The man's words faded as Nicole circled their small living room, peeking through the window toward Cari's designated parking spot on each pass. Empty. As it had been since last night. Nicole had received all the same advice and sentiments when she'd made her first call to the police department at two in the morning. The officer on duty then had encouraged her to get some sleep, claiming circumstances often looked different by light of day.

Currently, they did not.

Blakely squirmed in her playpen, probably sensing the tension rolling off her aunt in waves.

Nicole's eyes misted with fatigue and frustration as she paused to stroke her niece's round cheek.

She'd been eight years old when Cari was born. And remembered clearly how she'd looked the first time she set eyes on her, wrapped in a pink blanket, dark curls springing out in all directions. Wide brown eyes fixed on hers.

Cari had looked then exactly as her daughter did now.

"Thank you," Nicole said abruptly, interrupting the officer. "I'll call back in a few hours." The fierce protectiveness she'd felt every day as a big sister blazed to life once more. The police weren't ready to look for Cari, but Nicole was.

She set her phone aside and lifted her sweet niece into her arms. "It's okay," she cooed, stopping the infant's small fussy sounds. She cradled Blakely's warm little body against hers, and their dark brown locks mingled against her shoulder. Homes women looked a lot alike, but the similarities always stopped there. Cari was carefree and energetic, afraid of nothing and happy in a nearly contagious way. Nicole was pragmatic and steadfast, a troubleshooter by nature, and on occasion slightly harsher than necessary, which she didn't mind if it got the job done. Her mother had insisted their differences were what made them a formidable team.

It was time to find her teammate.

"How about a drive?" she asked Blakely. "Fresh air. Sunshine. Sound good?"

If she happened to discover her sister's car abandoned, or some other evidence to suggest Cari wasn't just being irresponsible, then the police would have to listen.

She buckled Blakely securely into her rear-facing car seat and thanked her stars she'd made the purchase. "Your mama wanted to save money by sharing a car seat," she told her, before pressing a kiss to the baby's forehead. "If I'd listened to her, she might've taken the seat with her last night. Then we'd be stuck at home instead of on our way to save her."

What she wouldn't give to have that argument with Cari again right now. She'd cheerfully fight about anything if it meant her sister was safe.

She climbed behind the wheel of her small gray SUV, and they were on their way.

Cari set her phone to Do Not Disturb while she worked, but always left the address where she could be found in case of an emergency. If her baby needed her, Nicole was to come straight to the source, etiquette be darned.

Not surprisingly, the GPS led them away from the valley, where single-family homes and apartment buildings peppered the landscape near a historic downtown. Warm southern sun heated her skin through open windows, while the balmy breeze did its best to ease her nerves. Coastal North Carolina was a sight to behold in every season, but their little inlet town was downright breathtaking in summertime. July was possibly the prettiest month of all.

They wound their way along the smooth black ribbon of road, past big white dairy barns and emerald fields, then upward, past miles of vibrant wildflowers and cookie-cutter neighborhoods into the mountains. Rugged, jutting rocks lined the road on one side, climbing into the sky, while a great precipice overlooked the sea on the other.

When houses appeared once more, they were massive and sprawling, nothing like the farmhouses and cottages of the working class, found closer to sea level. These properties were owned by folks who probably never got their hands dirty. If they did, there were luxurious in-ground and infinity pools waiting out back to wash away their cares.

Finally, the small voice on her phone announced their arrival, and Nicole slowed near a multilevel Frank Lloyd Wright knockoff on the corner of multiple entwining roads. It was a wonder residents ever learned their way around.

"This is it," she told Blakely, catching her eye in the baby mirror she'd attached to her car's back-seat headrest. Blakely chewed contentedly on one pudgy fist, her face reflected in the shiny silver plastic, then again in Nicole's rearview. "Your mommy was here last night. Working hard to buy you nice toys so you can chew on your fist instead."

Blakely hiccupped a laugh against her knuckles, and Nicole smiled.

None of the cars parked along the street were Cari's.

She circled the area once more with identical results.

Unease pooled and coiled in her core as she passed the house in question for a third time.

Cari had been fine before the fancy party. She'd come home and showered after her waitressing shift at a restaurant in town. She'd kissed Blakely goodnight a hundred times and promised to be home as soon as possible. Extra shifts and gigs at private parties had become part of her routine since Blakely's birth. And she'd taken full advantage of the free babysitting opportunities afforded by a sister who had the summer off from teaching second grade.

Nicole never minded. She loved the extra time with her niece, and seeing her sister thriving was a joy all on its own. Life hadn't always been this way for Cari.

She thought again of the short video Cari sent for Blakely. Nicole had replayed it several times throughout the night, but there were only notes of happiness in her voice and smile. No signs anything was amiss.

Aside from the video, Cari had sent a single picture of a small bridge illuminated in fairy lights. Presumably a landscaping feature in the homeowner's backyard. Something Cari would insist they make for Blakely somewhere, someday.

Nicole exhaled a heavy breath and pulled onto the home's double-wide driveway.

The garage door opened and a man stilled when he saw her exit the SUV. "Can I help you?" he asked.

"Yes. Hi," she said, opening the back door to gather Blakely into her arms. "I hope so." She stepped around her car, moving in the man's direction. "My sister worked at a party here last night. She hasn't come home, and I'm starting to worry. I thought you might remember her, or could put me in contact with the company you used for the catering. She was a member of the waitstaff."

His eyes widened slightly at the announcement Cari hadn't come home, then narrowed suspiciously when Nicole made her request. "I'm sorry. You must be mistaken. I haven't hired any catering company. Now, if you'll excuse me, I have to get to work." He dropped behind the wheel of his high-end sports car and drove away.

The garage door shut emphatically behind him.

She shook off the urge to retreat and marched to the home's front porch instead.

A phone rang somewhere inside while Nicole pressed the bell.

Long seconds passed before the clicking of heels carried to the door.

She stepped back as the great wooden barrier swept open, revealing a thin blonde in a fitted red dress, a pair of fawn-colored heels on her feet. "Can I help you?" she asked, fastening a golden hoop to one earlobe. Her skin was clear and tanned, her makeup flawless and her smile warm.

"Hello," Nicole said gently, putting on the voice and smile she used on parents and new students at the beginning of each school year. "I'm looking for my sister. She was part of the waitstaff at a party here last night, and I wondered if you could look at a photo of her and let me know if you remember seeing her?"

She freed her phone from one pocket and swiped quickly through saved images. "I understand if you didn't have time to meet every server, but it would mean a lot if you would just look. Or if you can tell me the name of the company you used to hire the servers."

She settled on an image of Cari with a wide-open smile and Blakely in her arms. "This is her. Her name is Cari Homes. She's twenty-three and—"

"No," the woman said sharply, smile fading as she scanned the street over Nicole's shoulders, probably looking for nosy neighbors. "There wasn't any party. I can't help you, and I didn't see your sister." Her gaze swept briefly to Blakely. "I'm sorry. I have to go," she added more softly, then stepped back and closed the door.

Nicole stared at the brass knocker, fighting the urge to rap it a few times, or maybe try the bell again. Instead, she turned, stunned silent, toward her car.

Blakely squirmed, and Nicole adjusted her niece in her arms. Blakely's fair baby skin was turning pink beneath the beating southern sun, and sunscreen hadn't crossed her aunt's harried mind.

"Poor sweetie," Nicole said, hurrying to secure her inside the car and out of the dangerous UV light.

It was possible Cari had written the address incorrectly, accidentally flipping two digits on the house number or misunderstanding the street name, but that seemed even more unlikely than the possibility nothing was wrong.

Unwilling to give up just yet, Nicole drove aimlessly through the neighborhood in search of Cari's car. She tried to imagine a scenario where Cari would lie about where she was last night but came up empty-handed.

When she wondered why a wealthy couple would lie about having a party, nothing good came to mind. She supposed it was possible the wife didn't know the husband had a party. Or maybe the call Nicole heard ringing while she'd waited on the doorstep was the husband instructing his wife to lie if she was questioned. Maybe they both knew something went wrong and were covering their backsides by pretending it hadn't happened.

The potential reasons were increasingly grim.

Nicole's chest constricted as she imagined gruesome accidents of every variety, and she pulled over to catch her breath. A small park caught her attention. A handful of kids played at its center, one of whom wore a coat that looked a lot like the one Cari had left home in the night before.

Nicole was out of her car in a heartbeat, pulling Blakely from her five-point safety harness and moving across the street at a clip. "Excuse me," she called, forcing a smile and waving an arm. "Hey! Hello!" She broke into a jog when the group looked her way.

The children ranged in age from ten or so to a pair of girls in their teens. They all stared as she approached. One of the younger girls wore the cropped lavender coat over a tank top with cutoff shorts and flip-flops.

"I'm Ms. Homes," she said. "I'm a teacher at Marshal's Bluff Elementary School. I think my sister lost her jacket. She was in this area last night, and it looks a lot like that one." She smiled at the young lady in question. "How long have you had that?"

The coat could belong to the girl, she supposed, but given the current temperatures, and her weather-appropriate outfit, otherwise, she doubted the kid had left home in a coat. Especially one clearly not her correct size.

The child looked at the teen, who raised her eyebrows in turn. "Fine," the kid said, sloughing off the coat. "I found it under a park bench and put it on. Purple is my favorite color, and no one else was around. I thought it was finders keepers."

"Which bench?" Nicole asked, fear gripping her chest as she reached for the coat.

The child pointed, and an anvil pressed against Nicole's lungs.

"Told you it was lost, dummy," another child scolded.

One of the teens shoved him in response. "Don't call names."

Nicole turned the jacket around in her hand, careful to keep Blakely secure as she looked. A small nail polish stain near the zipper sent her back to the day Cari had selected the coat and they'd gotten manicures together at the mall. She worked to press words through her tightened throat. This was her sister's coat. Why was it under a park bench? "Thank you."

The benches were all empty now, and the group of children moved away.

She hugged Blakely and clutched the jacket against

them both. "Where did you go?" she whispered into the day.

With a deep intake of air, she moved back toward her car, planting comfort kisses against her niece's head as they moved. Blakely smelled like love and hope. Nicole needed both, and Cari probably needed them more.

The sharp roar of an engine stopped her short of stepping onto the road. A sleek black sedan barreled past, engine growling. The vehicle turned the next corner with a piercing squeal of tires and disappeared.

Nicole shook away the rush of gooseflesh and foreboding that had appeared with the car, then ran to her SUV and secured Blakely in her car seat.

She pulled carefully away from the curb with a multitude of backward glances, praying her sister would appear. Somewhere on the fringe. Unharmed and oblivious to the lost time. Instead, she told her phone to direct her home.

Something dark flashed across her rearview mirror as she rolled forward, under command of her GPS.

The black car that had screamed past the park earlier was now behind her and quickly drawing near.

Nicole toed the gas pedal with increased purpose, stretching the space between them.

Blakely's eyes drooped in the reflection of her toy mirror, lulled by the heat of the day and the gentle rock of the SUV in motion.

The black car snarled loudly, reclaiming the little space Nicole had gained. It quickly matched her speed on the narrow curving roads. Tint on the windows, combined with glare from the sun, made the driver invisible, but everything about the moment felt pointed and intentional.

Nicole's speed edged higher, nearing ten miles over the posted limit, and she wondered if she should pull into someone's driveway. Maybe make a run for their front door. Would the other driver give chase on foot as well?

Was she being chased?

The time it would take to get Blakely into her arms, and the possibility no one would answer the door at a randomly selected home, tore her rattled heart into pieces. How could she escape this car?

The sudden growl of the vehicle's engine snapped her eyes to the rearview mirror in time to see the sedan lurch closer, slowing only when its front bumper disappeared.

Nicole cussed.

Blakely burst into tears. The engine noise and her aunt's outburst had apparently tipped the scales against her prospects for sleep.

"Sorry," Nicole chanted, her fingers painfully tight around the steering wheel. "Shh. It's okay."

The incredibly steep road back to town came into view. Light glinted off the sun-bleached rock face on her right, and danced over the inlet waters on her left, hundreds of feet below.

She braced to hold her ground as a final, teeth-rattling groan shot the black sedan forward and into the oncoming lane.

The driver darted in front of Nicole, causing her to swerve and slam the brakes before it zoomed away.

She eased into the next available space along the road's shoulder and cried with Blakely as the car's taillights vanished into the distance.

Nicole didn't have proof her sister was in trouble, or that the black sedan had just delivered a warning, but she knew in her bones both were true.

And there was only one man on earth who would believe her.

Chapter Two

Dean Beaumont fastened the latch on his tackle box and set it with the rest of the gear collecting on his front porch. Long, lazy summer Sundays spent fishing with his brother and business partner, Austin, were a tradition he enjoyed with increasing appreciation. This week, he craved the respite more than ever.

Folks always assumed being a private investigator in a town as small as Marshal's Bluff would be a bore. But there were awful people everywhere. Even in nice little towns where nothing ever seemed to happen. Because people were just like the waters he liked to fish on. Calm and inviting on the surface with a whole lot going on underneath.

He exhaled a long breath and readjusted the ball cap on his head. With a little luck there'd be a breeze on the harbor today, because he'd been outside for all of three minutes and already felt the familiar prickle of sweat beading across the back of his neck. According to the thermostat on his porch post, it was nearing ninety. It'd be even hotter on the water with the sun's rays reflected back at him from every direction.

He peered down the long gravel drive toward the main road, willing Austin's red-and-white Ford to appear. An apparition of heat hovered over the distant ground.

Austin was notorious for running late, but that never stopped Dean from worrying. Call it paranoia, or a protective instinct, but he doubted there'd ever be a day he didn't fear that the ugly things they investigated might come calling for his brother.

If Austin was on task, as he should've been, he'd delivered a pile of incriminating photos to an unfortunate client this morning. Definitive proof the client's spouse was cheating. It was one of their easier jobs. Because when a client suspected their significant other was stepping out on them, they were almost always right.

The downside was that jobs like these weren't exactly improving Austin's outlook on relationships or commitment. Which was something they could be talking about while fishing, if the knucklehead ever arrived.

The thought of failed commitments sent Dean's hand plunging into his pocket. A habit he'd developed a while back. His fingers found the penny with ease, and he relaxed by a small measure. He'd won the coin with a heart-shaped hole punched through it at a carnival and given it to his fiancée, Nicole, one balmy fall night. She'd kissed it and handed it back, telling him it was his, and he could carry her heart with him wherever he went. The coin had become a talisman. He never left home without it, though he hadn't spoken to her in more than a year.

He released the coin, unwilling to look too long or hard at why he couldn't leave the penny behind. Still, the memories of their demise poured back unbidden. He'd let his devastation over a child abduction case drive him half-mad when they were together, and he'd practically pushed her out the door when the missing boy's body was discovered. He'd shouldered that burden as if he were the cause, when he should've trusted her to help him process the pain.

He scrubbed a hand over his unshaven cheeks and headed inside for a tall glass of water. He poured, then drained the glass, wincing at the way it burned his tightened throat.

Then, finally, the sound of tires on gravel turned him toward the door.

He set the glass aside and cast his gaze over the small log cabin, double checking things before they left. Windows were shut. Stove burners off. Lunch was in the cooler.

The truck door closed before Dean reached the porch. He felt his brow wrinkle when the door closed again.

"What the heck took you so long?" he asked, swinging onto the porch with a smile.

But it wasn't Austin's truck in the driveway. Or his brother climbing the steps.

It was Nicole.

And a baby.

Dean's gaze jerked from Nicole's anguished face

to the tiny look-alike in her arms, and a string of un-intelligible sounds escaped his mouth.

"Dean," she said, voice strangled and gaze plead-ing. "I need your help."

He was at her side in the next heartbeat, ushering her into his home. "Of course. Here. Sit. I'll get you some water." He crossed to his kitchen several feet away and returned quickly with her drink. The flush in her cheeks and red in her eyes told him whatever had happened wasn't good. His heart pounded at the thought of her pain.

She sat on the edge of his couch, limbs trembling slightly as she lay the child on the cushion at her side.

"What's going on?" he asked. "What can I do?"

She accepted the drink and gulped it, visibly strain-ing against a breakdown.

His gaze strayed to the dark-haired baby with wide brown eyes and perfect curls. He'd cared for dozens of little ones, thanks to life on his parents' ranch, where troubled teens, often with children, stayed until their circumstances improved. Nicole's sister, Cari, had spent time on the ranch once, too. It was how he'd met Nicole.

The baby before him appeared to be four or five months old. Add nine months for a pregnancy, and the child must've been conceived while Dean and Ni-cole were together, though admittedly near their end.

"Nicole?" he pressed, panic welling in his chest. Not because he could be a father, but because Nicole was scared speechless, and suddenly it felt as if his entire world was at stake.

"My sister's missing," she said. "She's in trouble and no one will listen to me. I've been babysitting Blakely since yesterday, but Cari never came home. Her phone goes straight to voice mail. The police say more time has to pass before they open a case, but something is wrong." Her voice shook on the final word. "I can feel it. I didn't want to just show up here like this, but I don't know where else to turn. I'm trying to hold it together, so I won't scare her baby, but I know she can sense my stress." Her eyes turned cautiously toward her niece, and the child cried, as if on cue.

"Hey." Dean crouched before her and took the empty glass from her hands. "We can figure this out. It's going to be okay."

She swallowed audibly and pulled the baby back into her arms. "I'm so scared," she whispered. "It's been a long time since I've been this afraid."

"Well, you're with me now," he said gently. "I've got you. And... Blakely?"

She nodded.

Her niece. "I can't believe I didn't know Cari had a baby. You're an aunt."

Nicole's frail smile quivered. "Yeah."

Dean forced himself to refocus. He could regret all the things he'd missed in the past year later. Right now, Nicole needed his help. "Tell me what you know about the situation with Cari, and we'll think this through."

Nicole exhaled a shuddered breath, then began to tell her story.

Ten minutes later, Blakely was fast asleep in Dean's arms as he paced the small cabin's floor.

Nicole curled on the couch, clearly exhausted, her face in her hands.

"Finn's on the way," he said, tucking his cell phone back into his pocket. "He'll open an official case and help us get things started." Having a local detective for a brother came in handy from time to time.

"Thank you," she said, scanning him with wary eyes. "For all of this."

He followed her gaze to the baby. "Anytime."

"What do you think about the homeowners?" she asked. "They were being weird, right? Or am I over-thinking? I am a stranger who approached them without warning, asking about a missing person."

"I wasn't there, but it sounds like they might be hiding something," he said. "You're usually a good judge of character, shaken or not. If you think they seemed on edge, you're probably right. The reason might not have had anything to do with Cari, but maybe it did. Either way, it doesn't sound as if this pair were seasoned criminals. That works in our favor. The nervous ones either come clean or get caught faster."

Nicole straightened and met his eye. "Faster sounds good."

"Can I see the video you mentioned?"

Dean adjusted Blakely in his arms and prepared himself for potential bad news. Users and addicts were master manipulators, and Cari had struggled with sobriety once. She might not have checked all the boxes as an addict, but he suspected she would always be one temptation away from a free fall. And like every loved one of someone with substance abuse problems, Nicole wouldn't want to accept that her sister was using again. Even if the evidence was clear.

He pressed a kiss to the top of Blakely's head while he waited for Nicole to find the video. As the child of an addict, Dean knew a little something about the lifelong turmoil Blakely had ahead of her, if Nicole was wrong about Cari's sobriety. Dean and his biological brother, Jake, had been luckier than most, fostered, then adopted, by the Beaumonts while they were still young. The Beaumonts had made every right move to protect them.

Nicole would do the same for Blakely, but it would never completely eliminate the mark a parent's addiction left on the kids.

"Here." She stood before him, arm extended, her phone turned in his direction.

A video centered the screen. Laughter and chatter mingled with music in the background. Cari held the camera close. Her hair and makeup were done. Her eyes were clear and focused.

"Good night, sweet angel baby girl," she cooed. "Mommy's sorry she isn't there to tuck you in tonight, but she's got to take advantage of your auntie Nicole while she can." She grinned widely in the teasing, practiced way of younger siblings. "Dream sweet dreams until I get home to snuggle you up. I'll be there soon." Cari blew a kiss and the video ended.

"They were outside somewhere," Nicole said.

"There seemed to be a group of other women with her. All in black dresses. All hyped up and happy. I've watched the clip a dozen times, and nothing seems wrong. I tried freezing the frames and zooming in on the other faces, but it's too dark and blurry. And I don't know any of her friends anymore." She shook her head, as if casting the idea aside. "She basically doesn't have friends anymore. She has me and she has Blakely."

Dean wet his lips, preparing to tread gently. "You said they were catering a party?" The women had been dressed as if they were going out.

She nodded again. "Serving at a private party. Cari waitresses at the diner downtown, and she started taking one of these side jobs every week or so. She's paid in cash and asked to wear a simple black dress. No aprons or anything like that. She says the servers are told to blend. She's always home on time. And she always calls when she's on her way."

Nicole's composure cracked, and Dean pulled her against him with one arm, careful not to wake Blakely in the process.

His heart swelled at the feel of her, the scent of her, the warmth. He also felt her pain and would do anything to make it end.

His front door swung open, and Austin's voice filled the space. "Hey, whose SUV is—"

Nicole stepped away and wiped her eyes. "Hey, Austin."

His mouth opened, and for a single beat, he was silent. "Nicole?" His smile emerged, and he dived for her.

Dean backed up a few paces, shielding Blakely as his brother spun Nicole off her feet. "What are you doing here, gorgeous? Change your mind about this old man?" He thrust a thumb in Dean's direction, then stilled when he finally noticed the baby.

Austin's eyes widened as he looked from Blakely to Dean and back.

"She's not mine," Dean said, hit with an unexpected pang of regret. "This is Cari's baby. You remember Nicole's little sister."

His smile returned. "Of course I do. I love that girl. I can't believe she's a mama! How is she?"

"Missing." Nicole released the word on a sigh. "I'm here for help."

Dean shook off the hit of rejection that came with her words, reminding him she wasn't here for him. She just needed his help. Something he would never deny her. Then he delivered the quick facts on the matter to his brother.

"Did you call Finn?" Austin asked.

Before Dean could answer, Finn's truck pulled into the drive behind Austin's.

"Guess that answers that," he said, moving to open the door for their newest guest.

"Not my first rodeo," Dean said. In case Austin forgot this was exactly the sort of thing they did for a living.

Nicole greeted Finn with a hug. He'd worked this case once before, when Cari was a runaway in need of a detox and complete reboot on life. He'd found her with a small crowd of users and young people near the industrial section of town. Finn had recommended a facility for her rehabilitation and the Beaumont Ranch for some downtime once she was clean.

Dean's gut tightened with the realization that Nicole was reliving her worst nightmare.

"All right," Finn said, motioning Nicole to sit. "I know you probably don't feel like eating, but it sounds like you're running on no sleep, and I'm guessing you skipped your meals, too."

Austin ambled in Dean's direction, arms outstretched for the baby. "I'll take care of this little cowgirl, so you can make sandwiches."

Nicole smiled, and Dean frowned.

"Coming right up, I guess." He released Blakely into Austin's care, then gathered the ingredients for a few ham and cheese sandwiches and got to work.

"Did you get a look at the car?" Finn asked.

Nicole shook her head. "It was black. Ridiculously clean. Probably new. High end. Fast. It was behind me a while, but when it cut me off, it was out of sight in seconds."

Finn nodded. "We'll take a look at some images online."

Dean set a plate with stacked sandwich halves on the table, then poured a bag of chips into a bowl. "Let me grab my laptop."

He returned to the kitchen table and searched for fast cars in black to help her with recognition, then he narrowed the search to only include sedans in the newest models.

Nicole selected a sandwich half, then scrolled through the resulting images.

His brothers exchanged looks but didn't comment on whatever they were thinking.

"Cari sent a good-night video for Blakely," Dean said. "She looked good in the clip."

They nodded, picking up on the thing he didn't say. Cari had been sober, with no indication of intoxication or an otherwise diminished capacity. At least at the time of the video.

"Good," Finn said. "Consider the case officially opened. I'm heading back to the station to see what I can learn based on what you've told me." He grabbed another half sandwich from the pile and stood. "I'll keep you in the loop as things progress. You." He pointed to Nicole. "Rest. Then get a list together of anyone you think might know something you don't about your sister. Hangouts. Interests. New people in her life. Old acquaintances making reappearances." He held her gaze for a long beat.

No one wanted to think Cari would make terrible choices at this point in her life, or that she would risk everything when she had a daughter to care for, but everyone in the room knew things happened, and humans didn't always make the right choices. Even the best of them.

Finn released her from his stare and tipped his hat before seeing himself out.

Blakely whimpered, and Nicole stood to relieve Austin.

"She's having a rough day," she said. "I can take her."

Austin turned away, an expression of exaggerated offense on his face. "I've got her. You eat. Rest. Talk things out with your man." He winked, and Dean made a mental note to throttle him.

That plan changed when Nicole walked straight into his arms and held on tight.

He wrapped her up protectively and pressed a gentle kiss against her head. "We're going to find your sister."

Chapter Three

Nicole climbed into the passenger seat of her SUV while Dean secured Blakely in the back. Asking for his help had been easy. Cari needed it. Letting him step in and ease Nicole's burdens was something else. She'd learned years ago, when Cari was at her worst, and their parents were either fighting or sobbing, not to be one more person in need. But Dean and his family were wired to get involved, however they could, whenever needed. And she'd never been so thankful for those qualities. It was no wonder he'd once meant everything to her. He was the perfect hero.

If only he'd learned to be a partner, too. She appreciated his big, giving heart, but she couldn't settle for anyone who refused to be her teammate.

At least the Beaumont brothers were working together to find Cari. She could never thank any of them properly for that.

Nicole took a few slow, cleansing breaths to re-center herself. Giving in to her heightened emotions when so much was at stake felt unreasonably self-ish. It was time to get her head together and think of ways to help the Beaumonts. But when she'd arrived on Dean's doorstep unannounced, asking for help, and he'd immediately accepted, she'd begun to feel herself unravel. He hadn't even waited to hear what she needed. He'd just brought her and Blakely into his home, then started giving. And it was as if a dam had broken loose inside her.

"Ready?" Dean asked, shifting into Reverse.

"Yes." She met his eyes with gratitude when further words failed.

They rode in companionable silence for several long minutes, heading back to the neighborhood where Cari had worked the night before.

"You doing okay?" he asked, eyeing her carefully as they made the ascent along the water.

She nodded, but her stomach clenched. "Actually, no," she admitted. "All this fear is triggering old memories. Part of me is trying to be angry, doubting her word about the job and address. Which is nonsense. She isn't that person anymore. And I kind of hate myself for having such awful thoughts."

The SUV leveled out at the top of the hill, rolling slowly to a stop sign inside the high-class neighborhood.

"Don't beat yourself up. That's normal," he said. "You lived in fear of losing her for years, and on the surface, today looks a lot like all those times before. You're experiencing the same emotions. Your brain is being flooded with all the same signals. It's trying to make sense of things by connecting this to old patterns."

Nicole wet her lips and nodded. More than one counselor had told her similar things over the years. "Is it ridiculous that I'm also feeling guilty for being so upset? I keep thinking if I'm this scared, how terrified is Cari? I'm still safe. My world is stable. But I still can't stop shaking."

"Your world is upside down," he countered. "Her traumas have always been your traumas, too. They always will be. She's your sister."

Nicole wiped a renegade tear from her cheek and concentrated on steadying her breaths.

"Nicole?" Dean said softly.

Her name on his tongue was nearly enough to crack her newly rebuilt composure.

"Did I make it worse?" he asked, sneaking peeks at her as he drove.

"No." Dean always made everything better. "Thank you for the reminder," she said. "And for being here."

Emotion rolled over his handsome features. "Where else would I be?"

Soon they passed the home where Nicole had knocked earlier, but Dean didn't stop. He made several loops through the winding streets, examining this world through sharp, trained eyes.

Nicole looked pointlessly for Cari's car, still nowhere to be found. "I can't decide if I'm more afraid she never made it here, or that she just never made it home from here. Without her car in the area, it makes me wonder if the people I spoke to really never saw her."

What if there wasn't a party? She dragged anxious fingers through her hair, hating the thoughts of doubt. "I know she was here," she said, as much to herself as to Dean.

"I believe you," he said. "And we believe Cari. Can you point me to the park you mentioned?"

Two turns later they pulled against the curb where Nicole had parked earlier.

"Here," she said. "I thought this was someone's backyard at first, but there are benches. And a group of kids were here." She twisted on her seat to fish Cari's coat from the floor of the back seat. "This is the coat I told you about."

Dean settled the SUV's engine and gave the lavender jacket a thorough exam.

Nicole had already done the same. No obvious damage. No hidden pockets or other places the destination of her whereabouts might be concealed.

She returned the item to the back seat when he finished.

"Okay. Next step." He opened his car door and smiled. "Let's see what else we can find in the park."

With Blakely in tow, they crossed the street and began a methodical search.

Dean peeked under every bench, carefully running his hand through the lush green grass.

Nicole turned in a slow circle, acclimating herself to the surroundings. "The party house is on top of that hill," she said. "If something frightened Cari and she left, moving downhill also makes sense. Town is downhill. So is the police station. Home. Safety."

Dean stretched onto his feet and rested both hands

on his hips. "Agreed." He fixed his eyes on the horizon and whispered into the heated air. "Where did you go next, Cari Homes?"

Nicole had asked the universe same thing.

And still there wasn't an answer.

DEAN WATCHED NICOLE with her niece, hating that there wasn't more he could do for either of them. Missing persons cases took time. They'd started early, which was good, but they had little to go on. And from the looks of the ladies in front of him, they could both use some rest.

He rubbed his palms together, fingers outstretched. "What do you say about getting out of the sun? Maybe taking the little one home. Cooling off. Getting some rest. Waiting for input from Finn and Austin. Maybe having a look in Cari's room?"

Nicole's brows rose and relief softened the tension in her face and shoulders. "I think that sounds really good. Blakely's been on the go all day. She should be in her bed for naps. Someplace familiar and comforting."

"Well, then," he said, spinning the key ring on one finger. "Point me to your home."

The look of appreciation on Nicole's face each time he expressed the smallest kindness was enough to break his heart. Didn't she know she deserved so much more? Kindness wasn't even the tip of the iceberg.

He drove back through the quiet tree-lined streets, then began the descent into town with a heavy heart.

Missing persons cases always took a toll on him, and leaving Cari's last known location empty-handed felt a lot like defeat.

Nicole kneaded her hands in her lap, probably feeling the same.

Dean set his fingers over hers on instinct, and she stilled. He stiffened slightly in response, having momentarily forgotten he had no right to touch her anymore. No claim to this access. Still, pulling away now could feel like rejection, and she hadn't immediately shaken him off.

He cleared his throat and gave her hand a gentle squeeze. "We'll figure this out." He'd said something similar before, and he would repeat the words as many times as she needed. He would find her sister.

"Thank you."

In cases like this one, things generally didn't get dicey until three days or more had passed. There was still room for hope. With some persistence and a little luck, Cari could be back safely long before then. "When we get to your place, we can reach out to Finn and Austin. See if they have anything."

"I still have Finn's number," Nicole said. "I can text him now."

Dean nodded. Contacting Finn would give her something to do, which would make her feel less powerless. And the reminder a local detective was actively working the case would be a bonus, even if he hadn't learned anything new.

Dean opened his mouth to say her suggestion sounded good, but a small sound escaped her. Prickles of foreboding climbed Dean's neck and arms. "What is it?"

She pointed to the windshield, indicating an oncoming vehicle still too distant to be more than a silhouette. "That's the car."

He frowned, straining to make out the details as it rumbled nearer.

"That sound," she said, rubbing gooseflesh from her skin. "I don't think I'll ever forget it."

The late-model Dodge Charger flew past them at double the speed limit. No plates, dark tint, just like she'd described earlier. And the signature engine growl was one enthusiasts worked long and hard under the hood to perfect. A glance in his side-view mirror revealed a hint of brake lights before the car zoomed away.

"What do we do?" she asked, voice thick with fear.

"Let Finn know we saw the car. It's a late-model Dodge Charger. He and local law enforcement can keep an eye out for it. See where it's spotted and who's driving. Meanwhile, we'll head to your place as planned."

She twisted in her seat, checking on Blakely before facing forward once more. She dug her phone from her purse. "It's not the same car I saw the guy at the house get into. Do you think that means anything?"

"Maybe," Dean said. Though at this point nothing was off the table for theories. "Did you get a look in the garage when the door went up?" There could easily have been two, possibly three other cars inside.

"No." She exhaled softly. "I was only thinking

of Cari. Maybe even hoping she'd bounce into view apologizing for scaring me. As if she might've been working, then fallen asleep in a spare bedroom, and the family was just too nice to wake her."

Before he could turn an encouraging smile her way, the Charger reappeared. This time in his rear-view mirror. "You should probably pass the information on to Finn."

Nicole's wide eyes were already on the mirror. "Okay."

The car roared closer, riding their bumper along the two-lane road above the water. The experience, given the infant in the back seat, Nicole at his side and a single lane separating them from a plummet into the sea, was genuinely terrifying.

The battered guardrail had never looked so flimsy. The barrier would be useless if the other driver chose to ram their SUV.

"We're on Highway 12," Nicole said into her phone, apparently having called Finn rather than texting. "Coming back from the address I gave you this morning."

Dean gauged the car's distance and considered his options as town drew near. "Tell him the engine's been souped up. Heavy tint. No other identifying features."

She repeated his words as the road angled away from the sea, cutting through fields and farmland instead of rock and mountain. "I'm putting you on speaker."

Finn repeated the description of the car for clarification while Dean began a series of turns and switchbacks when other roads became available. A procedure designed to lose their tail.

Nicole confirmed the description, and Dean took another wild turn.

"We're almost to the high school," he said, projecting his voice in the direction of the phone. "He's on us like a bumper sticker."

"Head toward the precinct," Finn advised. "I'll move your way. Don't let him rattle you. Mind your speed."

Dean fought the urge to remind his younger brother he'd learned to give advice like that from Dean. At thirty-four, he was hardly a novice prone to panic. "I've got this," he said instead. "Just get out here and do your lights and sirens thing."

Nicole raised the phone as she peered behind them. "I knew this guy was a threat, or at least a message the first time he followed me. There are plenty of other vehicles on the road to torment. He's chosen mine twice."

The car gave a louder, more menacing growl and launched into the oncoming lane, then in front of the SUV, barely avoiding a head-on collision with a pickup. A moment later the car was gone, vanished into the distance as quickly as it had appeared on their tail.

Nicole stifled a scream, and Blakely burst into tears.

"What happened?" Finn barked.

"We lost our tail," Dean said. "Too many witnesses, maybe."

"Or," Nicole panted, dropping her fingers from her chest to tap against her phone screen, "he saw me recording him."

Dean's lips quirked into a smile. "You got that on video?"

"Yep."

"Good thinking," Finn said. "I'm going to need that file."

She composed her features into a satisfied grin. "Already done."

DEAN SENT HER a look of unfiltered pride, then took a long, convoluted route to Nicole and Cari's apartment, assuring the Charger didn't manage to follow or find them.

Blakely calmed with some soothing comfort from her aunt.

Nicole had always been a troubleshooter and quick thinker. Those characteristics had likely paid off today in droves. Video of the car would go a long way in helping Finn nail down the driver or owner. He couldn't imagine how she'd remained calm when it'd been her behind the wheel, especially considering she'd just realized her sister was missing and something strange was going on. A strong testament to her grit and character.

They parked outside a three-story apartment building and made their way to the front. A single camera pointed at the parking lot and street.

An older gentleman paused to hold the door open for them on his way out.

"Thanks," Nicole said, moving swiftly inside.

"Did you know him?" Dean asked, hating the ridiculous lack of security.

She stuck her key in a first-floor apartment door lock. "No. Why?"

"Do you think he recognized you, or knows you live in the building? Do you know your neighbors?"

She frowned. "Probably not, and maybe," she said. "Everyone keeps to themselves here. It's mostly working couples. A few older folks, but it's usually pretty desolate during the workday." She swung the door open and motioned him inside. "This is it."

He gave the long, quiet hallway a final look before stepping inside. The small space had an open floor plan, much like his cabin. An island bar separated the kitchen and living room. A hall led from the main hub, presumably to the bedrooms and a shared bath. The decor was inviting and overrun with charm.

"It's not usually this clean," she said. "I couldn't sleep last night, so I scrubbed everything while I waited for Cari to call or show up."

Dean snorted softly. "Most people tell folks to excuse the mess, when there's obviously nothing out of place."

She rolled her eyes. "Yeah, well, our place is usually a disaster. Especially during the school year. Cari works nights after I get home, so Blakely never has to go to day care. She can't afford it, and everything is covered in germs there. We basically run in circles just trying to care for the baby and get where we need to be on time. No one here has had a full night's sleep in six months."

"Is that Blakely's age?" he asked, reevaluating the little girl. Was she a couple of months older than he'd guessed?

Nicole deftly prepared a bottle in the kitchen, cradling Blakely in her opposite arm. "She'll be five months this week. But Cari was on bed rest for most of her last trimester. This kiddo was in a big hurry to meet me, I guess." She moved to the couch and rested her niece on her lap, then slid the bottle's nipple into Blakely's mouth with a smile. "We thought we were going to lose her for a while. Then, one day the time was finally up, and here she is."

"And she's perfect," Dean said, enjoying her story and the love evident in her voice.

"Absolutely."

"Sounds like the three of you have been through a lot together," Dean said.

Tears welled in Nicole's eyes as she dragged her gaze away from Blakely. "What if Cari doesn't… What if she's already…"

Dean moved to Nicole's side and crouched before her. "It's not time to think like that. If we get evidence to suggest you should prepare for the worst, I'll be straight with you. I promise. But we aren't there yet. Not even close. Your sister is a fighter and a survivor. Just like you."

Nicole's expression hardened, and she rose with the baby. Her shoulders squared, and her spine straightened. "You're right. We need to keep going."

Dean stretched onto his feet beside her. "Where are we going?"

"To her room." Nicole moved into the hallway. "I'm not going to love doing this, but we should search Cari's things."

He followed her with a fresh jolt of purpose. This was what he did best. "Any chance she left her laptop?"

"On her desk." Nicole opened the device and stepped aside, giving Dean room to work.

"Perfect." He hunched over the lock screen, fingers resting on the keys. "Any guesses about the password?" If not, he doubted it would take long to crack. Most people weren't very creative.

"Try heart of hearts," she said. "Capital *H*s and a zero for the *o* in *of.* That was the password when she was still pregnant. I used her laptop at the hospital. If she was feeling really clever, she might've used threes in place of the *E*s."

Dean tried the suggested passwords, and Cari's desktop appeared. "Looks like she was feeling clever."

Nicole smiled and moved Blakely into position at her shoulder. She patted the baby's back and shifted foot to foot. "Now what?"

"Now we see what she's been up to online. Find out what she's researched. Who she talked to. What they said." Dean accessed the device's browsing history and opened a few web pages. "Looks like she's still logged into her email and social media accounts. That'll save us some time."

"Good," Nicole said. "So why are you frowning?"

He did his best to clear his expression, then angled the device in her direction. There were at least a dozen recent exchanges between Cari and a guy whose profile image involved a crude hand gesture and a lolling tongue. "Who's Mikey Likey?"

"Ugh. Her ex." Nicole peered over his shoulder at the screen. "She dated him before meeting Blakely's dad. She and Mikey stayed friends."

"And Blakely's dad?" Dean asked.

"Became vapor the minute two lines appeared on the pregnancy test."

Dean bit back his opinion on anyone who'd abandon their baby and her mother. Instead, he doubled down on the task at hand. "Then let's start with Mikey."

Chapter Four

Nicole curled on the couch after dinner, eyes fixed on the clock. Tension only slightly eased from a long cry in a steaming-hot shower. She'd fed and bathed Blakely, then helped her fall asleep for the night. Now the apartment was still, aside from the tick of the clock's second hand.

There were no new leads on Cari.

And she'd been chatting regularly with Mikey. A terrible influence from her past. Why? And what else was going on in Cari's life that Nicole didn't know?

"Hey," Dean said, taking the seat beside her and offering a mug of steaming tea. "You still like lavender and vanilla. The cupboard's full of it."

She smiled. "There was a sale."

Dean used to bring her a cup when she stayed up late grading art projects and worksheets from her classroom.

"Thanks." She held the tea beneath her nose to inhale the soothing scents. It was time to refocus. Think of something that could help the Beaumonts make headway in finding her sister.

But her tired, desperate mind had lost its clarity, and Blakely would be awake and hungry before dawn.

Dean sipped from his mug, the contents of which smelled distinctly like black coffee, and guilt tugged at her heart once more. She'd taken him away from Sunday fishing without any notice. He looked forward to the time with his brother, alone on the lake. He'd once told her those trips helped him re-center himself after a long week of turbulence. But this week, she'd barged in needing help. Then she'd monopolized the rest of his day, and the foreseeable future, with her problem. And guilty or not, she couldn't bring herself to tell him he could go home if he wanted. She prayed he didn't want to, because she was holding on to sanity by a thread, and his presence was making her whole impossible situation survivable.

Blakely deserved at least one adult who wasn't falling apart.

The thought of other adults sat Nicole upright. She'd been putting off the inevitable all day, and she couldn't wait any longer.

Dean lowered his mug and furrowed his brow.

"I have to call Mom." She set her tea aside and dropped her face into waiting palms. "I didn't want to have to make this call. Every time I've thought about it, I decided to wait a little longer, hoping I wouldn't have to do it at all." Cari had been gone for twenty hours. "She's going to be a mess, and there's no one to comfort her. Plus she's sure to be upset with me for waiting so long to tell her." Nicole lifted her head and turned tired eyes to meet Dean's. "Making this

call means this is all real. And I really, really don't
want it to be."

He rubbed a palm over her back, smoothing the
soft cotton of her T-shirt, offering companionship
instead of words. "Why doesn't she have anyone?"
Dean asked. "What about your dad?"

Nicole's last bit of energy seemed to drain. Apparently a lot could happen in a year. "Mom moved to
Charleston a few months ago to take care of her parents. Grandpa had a stroke and they needed to hire
a caretaker but couldn't afford one. Mom was struggling financially after the divorce, so moving in with
my grandparents has helped all three of them. She
misses us, but she's glad to be able to do this for her
folks. She calls most nights around ten."

According to the clock, that was in less than an
hour.

Dean twisted on the couch for a better look at her.
"Your folks got divorced? I'm sorry to hear that."

She sighed. "I want to say me too, but I don't know."

Cari's teenage issues had taken a toll on everyone and strained the family in a dozen ways. Their
mom had internalized it, wondering where she'd gone
wrong as a mother and how she'd failed Cari. Their
father had grown distant, unwilling to show or deal
with his pain.

Eventually, Cari put her life back together, but their
parents' marriage had broken irrevocably. That was
the thing most people didn't realize. Drugs crushed
everyone in their reach. The waves and ripples of pain
went out in long arcs, breaking up friendships, driv-

ing away peripheral people and annihilating support systems for everyone in the family.

"He remarried," Nicole added. "They have a baby a little older than Blakely."

Dean's brows rose. "How long have they been divorced?"

"Not long enough for them to have a baby Tony's age. Dad and Heidi eloped a few months after he moved out. We learned about her and the coming addition to our family in the same conversation."

"Wow."

"That's what we said, too." Nicole smiled. "There was also a little cussing."

Dean laughed. "I guess so."

"Once Tony was born, Dad sent photos and confessed to meeting his new wife while he was still with Mama. He blamed her for pulling away in their time of crisis. He thought she'd prioritized Cari's situation over his needs and their marriage, so he was forced to find comfort elsewhere."

Dean's mouth turned down and his eyes flashed hot.

Nicole sighed. "I should probably call Dad, too."

"Why don't you let me call him?" Dean suggested. "He knows me well enough, and I can relay anything he needs to know. Tell him you're with Blakely right now if he asks for you. You can concentrate on that call to your mama."

"Would you?" Her words caught in her throat, and she blew out a long shaky breath.

"I've got this. Text me his number."

Nicole did as Dean asked, grateful for a partner in this moment and glad to skip that particular call.

She dialed and waited. Dean did the same.

When her mom's voice mail picked up, Nicole was equally sorry and relieved. She left a message in her most casual tone possible and asked her to return the call.

Dean pursed his lips. "No answer. I didn't leave a message. I thought a voice mail from me might tip him off to the problem, and I heard you leaving a message for your mama. I'll try again in an hour."

She returned to her tea, taking several long sips as she unwound. "I can't believe Cari kept in touch with Mikey. I know that's the least of our problems right now, but I'm truly stunned. He played a big part in some of the worst days of her life. Why would she want to talk to him? And why would she keep it from me? I guess this is my answer. Look at how judgmental I'm being."

"You're upset," Dean said. "Give yourself a break. We'll know more after he responds to your message. If he doesn't respond by morning, we'll go find him."

"Okay." That seemed reasonable, and it gave her a new purpose. Tomorrow they would look for Mikey.

A few hours ago she'd typed three little words into the chat box on Cari's laptop.

Can we talk?

She hadn't let him know it was her. With a little luck he'd agree to meet her somewhere, then she and

Dean could corner him for information. Instead of giving him the chance to simply stop responding.

"Your sister's going to be okay," Dean said softly, apparently seeing where her mind had gone. "She's tough, smart and resourceful. Finn and Austin are chasing leads. You and I will keep caring for her little girl and pulling any thread we find."

Nicole turned on the cushion, tucking her feet beneath her and leaning against his side. Greedy for a little of his strength and assurance. "I felt like I failed her as a big sister when I found out she was using. I blamed myself for not seeing the signs. And I kept that up right through her time at your family's ranch. I'm feeling exactly that way again now. I didn't think I ever would."

Dean's arm looped around her shoulders, pulling her in close. "I know." He held her silently while she worked her way through the tea. When she set the empty mug on the coffee table, he offered an encouraging smile. "Aside from becoming World's Best Aunt, what have you been up to this year?"

Nicole smiled, glad for the mental and emotional break. "I'm still teaching at the elementary school, and I still love it. Half my wardrobe has glitter in places it will never come out. I helped Cari through her last trimester. I was her birthing coach through a pretty traumatic labor and delivery. Saw things I'll never unsee." She slid her eyes to Dean.

He laughed.

"And now I've got this perfect little niece. My sister is a wonderful mom. She's become my best friend.

It's the closest we've ever been, and I've been really happy."

The eight-year age difference between them had made a relationship on any kind of equal ground nearly impossible until Cari became a mom. She'd still been a kid when Nicole was in high school. She'd still been learning to drive when Nicole had graduated from college and started teaching. What they'd created this year was real, and it hurt all the more to lose her now.

"I'm glad y'all found your ways to each other," Dean said. "I've always liked Cari. Lots of people take wrong turns in life, but I knew the moment your folks brought her to the ranch she was going to be okay."

"Thanks." She smiled. "What about you?" Nicole asked, realizing for the first time that Dean could be married or engaged, or even have a baby of his own in the time they'd been apart. They'd barely spoken about anything other than Cari's disappearance, and suddenly she wanted to know everything. Especially the parts about a potential love interest or child. "What did I miss in your life this year?"

Dean stilled for a long beat, and Nicole found herself doing the same. "I've been working through some things," he said finally. "It took me a while to find my way back after you left, but for what it's worth, I know you were right for leaving. I let that case and that family's tragedy derail everything in my life. It wrecked me, and that hurt everyone who loved me. Not to mention all the cases I had to turn down while

I got myself together. I wasn't helping anyone else who needed help. Thankfully, I've probably got the best support system on earth, and I figured things out eventually."

Nicole had been part of his system once. Maybe she'd failed him by walking away when he was at his worst, but knowing the strides she'd made with Cari these last few months, it was hard to want to change anything about the way things had gone. And selfish as it felt, Nicole stood by her reason for leaving. She wanted a partner in all things, and Dean had stopped letting her in. He'd pulled away in his pain just like her dad, and look at how that had ended.

"I'm glad you're okay, Dean," she said. "And I'm really thankful you're here."

"Me, too."

NICOLE GROANED AND SHIFTED, sore from a restless night on her couch. Shafts of light through her living-room curtain stung her tired eyes.

Sounds of movement somewhere in the apartment set her heart and mind on alert.

For the briefest moment, she thought Cari and Blakely were sharing breakfast or playing together.

Then the previous day came crashing back.

Dean's muffled voice slowly reached her on the still morning air, and she pushed herself onto her feet.

She gripped and kneaded the aching muscles along her neck and shoulders where tension and a night on the couch bit and cramped them. Exhaustion had pulled her under, but she'd barely slept during the eight hours that had passed.

Blakely must've been awake for nearly three.

Nicole padded down the hallway to Cari's room, where Dean paced the carpet, a cell phone pressed to one ear. Blakely rocked in her front carrier, attached to his broad chest. A pink pacifier bobbing double time in her little rosebud mouth.

Cari's normally cluttered space was tidy. Her things organized and stacked in neat piles along the wall and on her bed.

Dean had inventoried her room.

He turned when she arrived in the open doorway. "Good morning."

"Hey." She forced a smile, taken aback by the wave of emotions. Seeing him in her apartment was strange. Seeing him with a baby in a front carrier was something else altogether. And seeing her little sister's room processed as if it was a crime scene was enough to make her stomach bottom out.

Dean wet his lips and turned slightly away. "Nicole's up. Keep me posted." He ended the call and tucked his phone into the pocket of his jeans.

Blakely cooed and babbled. Her wide brown eyes danced with pleasure, enjoying two of her most favorite things at once: her pacifier and being carried.

"She woke at dawn, so we've been hanging out," he explained. "Were you able to rest on the couch? I thought about carrying you to your bed, but that seemed—" He cringed. "And I didn't want to wake you, so…"

Memories of being carried to bed by Dean stunned her brain momentarily, fully eliminating any fog that had remained after a restless sleep. "I'm okay," she said. "Thank you for caring for Blakely. And doing all this." She motioned to the room. "How's that going?"

"I don't know her like you do, so nothing stood out to me as unusual. But I've organized as much as I can to make it easier for you to take a look and see what you think."

"That's good, I think," Nicole said. "I'll look as soon as I've had some coffee. I don't want to miss anything. Do you want some?"

Dean lifted a small stack of papers from Cari's desk. "Sounds good. I wanted to show you these. I found them hidden inside the album covers of her old vinyl record collection."

Nicole's heart stuttered, her outstretched hand frozen a few inches from Blakely before she regained herself enough to carry the motion through. She stroked her niece's chubby cheek and planted a kiss on her head before stepping back. She met Dean's steady gaze with utter fear. "What is it?"

"Five college acceptance letters."

Nicole blinked. Of all the things he could've said, this was at the bottom of her expectations. "Colleges?"

He passed her the findings with a shy smile. "All sent in the last two months."

The papers were heavy in Nicole's grip. Cari hadn't told her about this, either. "I had no idea she was thinking about going to college. Or that she'd applied."

Her attention moved to the top line of each letter.

Congratulations Carolyn Homes! We're hon-
ored to announce your acceptance for enroll-
ment in the fall semester.

"She got in," Nicole repeated, sifting through the pages. "Everywhere."

Dean's hands covered hers as they began to shake. "Cari was planning a better future. The extra cater-ing jobs she took were probably meant to help with tuition. And maybe this was going to be a surprise."

Nicole's gaze snapped back to Dean's. Her sis-ter wanted to go to college. She wasn't falling into trouble with old connections. She was rising above her challenges, like she always did. "We need to talk to Mikey."

Chapter Five

It was nearing lunchtime when Dean and Nicole finally left the apartment with Blakely. Nicole's sweet
little niece had fallen asleep while the adults had
breakfast, and neither of them wanted to wake her.
Instead, they'd drifted into easy conversation that
had reminded Dean how much he'd missed talking
with her. Nicole was intuitive and kind in ways most
people weren't, and her levelheaded approach to life
was something he could use more of.

She strapped Blakely into the rear-facing car seat,
then took the seat at Dean's side, allowing him to drive
her SUV again. "Ready."

Dean waited while she buckled up, then reversed
out of the parking lot and onto the residential streets
of her neighborhood. The hot summer sun beat down
on the pavement, creating an apparition of heat over
the asphalt.

He needed to make a pit stop at his place. He hadn't
expected to spend the night at Nicole's, and he needed
some basic things, like a change of clothes and his own

toiletries. "Care if we swing back by my house after this?"

Thankfully Nicole had provided an unopened toothbrush, but his deodorant was pushing the boundaries of its advertised twenty-four-hour protection.

"Of course." She looked nearly as exhausted as she had last night, despite the hours of rest on her couch.

Dean made a mental note to create an opportunity for her to sleep again soon.

Aside from the tension rolling off her in waves, Nicole looked as beautiful as ever. She'd hidden warm brown eyes behind mirrored sunglasses, and her thick dark hair fell over her shoulders in matching French braids. She wore a simple blue tank top that hugged her curves and jean shorts that would've been his undoing in any other situation.

She caught him staring, and he returned his attention to the road.

"Where are we going?" she asked. "The police station? The diner where Cari works?"

Dean adjusted his grip on the wheel, bracing for what he was about to say. "I thought we'd start down by the docks."

Nicole stilled, and her gaze flickered to the window.

Marshal's Bluff law enforcement had recovered Cari from the docks when she'd gone missing years ago. She'd been high and sleeping on the concrete beneath highway overpasses as if she were homeless, instead of breaking her entire family's hearts.

Dean helped locate missing people in similar situations every month, but he hadn't been to the docks in some time. Local police frequently set the homeless community on the move, attempting to get as many as possible into shelters and return the runaways to their families. Eventually, the group always reunited in a new location. Or in one of their previously vacated favorites.

For most folks, it was probably hard to believe Marshal's Bluff had a homeless population or any amount of addicts. The streets were clean, crime was low, and the town was inarguably charming. But anywhere there were people, there were problems.

They motored along residential roads toward the sea, eventually trading houses for small businesses and cafés in the picturesque downtown. Historic and postcard-perfect, the blocks from Main to Bayview were pristine, lined with trees and doused in an abundance of cheerful potted plants.

Several blocks and one turn later, large utilitarian buildings rose from the concrete, turning the quaint, colorful surroundings gray and sparse. Scorching sunlight glinted off harbor waters, and exhaust rose from ships and semitrucks delivering large-scale shipments.

The types of pedestrians changed with the scenery. No more couples holding hands and smiling singles walking dogs or families pushing strollers. In this area of town, individuals stood on corners looking defeated, lost or angry, often staring down commuters who dared drive past. Some were lookouts, watching for signs of the authorities while their counterparts engaged in unsavory or illegal activities. Others were just getting by, passing time without purpose or plan. By night, these blocks weren't safe for anyone without a connection to the various crimes or a weapon for protection.

Dean always traveled with both. "I've got a few contacts down here, but they don't spend a lot of time with the community we're going to talk to," he explained, scanning the area for a place to start asking questions. "We'll reach out to them next if this is a bust."

The highway overpasses came into view, and Dean slowed to a crawl. The bridges offered shade and acted as a hub for those folks with nowhere to go while the rest of the world was on the clock.

Nicole straightened as they reached the edge of the first bridge.

The sidewalks were lined in trash and makeshift shelters. A mass of young people meandered in the grassy space beyond the road.

"Do you think she could be here?"

"No." Dean covered her hand with his and offered a squeeze. "But I'm hoping Mikey is, or someone will know where we can find him."

He parked the SUV along the curb and climbed out.

Nicole followed suit, sliding Blakely into a sling on her hip.

Several people took notice immediately. Some standing taller, as if they might want trouble. Others appeared frightened, clearly unsure what to make of the newcomers. Dean reached for Nicole's hand and glanced at her to be sure he hadn't overstepped. "Okay?"

She nodded.

His gaze jumped back to the appraising groups. None of the wary or hostile faces looked like Mikey's profile photo.

Dean rolled his shoulders back and flattened his expression, then raised his cell phone, Cari's image already on-screen. "We're looking for a missing woman. She used to come down here a few years ago. Her name's Cari," he told the group.

Mentioning Cari's former affiliation with the area softened a few faces and gained the interest of others.

He extended the phone in their direction as he walked slowly past. "She's been gone more than a day now. Her family's worried. She stays in touch with Mikey, and we thought someone here might know where we can find him."

An older woman with a long gray ponytail and scar along one cheek stepped forward. "How do you know Mikey?"

"We don't," Nicole said. "But he's Cari's friend, and I'm hoping he can help me find her. She's my little sister, and I'm scared. I don't know what else to do."

The crowd shifted and murmured. Several people dropped back, interest lost.

A trio of men Dean guessed was the group's muscle lined up and moved in his direction.

The older woman outstretched an arm at her side, palm up, stopping them in their places. "Cari with the stars on her wrist?" she asked. "Young. Short hair. Fancy life?"

Nicole exhaled a shuddered breath, and Dean

squeezed her hand again. "Yes," she croaked. "She's twenty-three now. Her hair is long, and she's put on weight. This is her daughter. I was babysitting when she went missing."

The woman examined Blakely from several feet away. "Mikey said she got clean."

"She did." Nicole nodded and sniffled, voice wavering. "She's my best friend and a really, really good mother."

Dean gritted his teeth against the lump rising in his throat. Nicole and her family had been through so much already. He hated that fate had brought them back here again. And he couldn't do a darn thing about it.

"She catered a party on the night she went missing," Nicole pressed. "Do you know anything about that?"

The woman shook her head. "No, but Mikey delivers pizzas for the place on Main Street with a rocket on the logo. Sometimes he comes by and brings food."

"Thank you," Nicole said.

The light in her eyes dimmed as she looked at Dean, and he knew what she was thinking without having to ask.

He removed his wallet from his pocket, tucking the cell phone away. "There's a ranch outside town where Cari spent a few weeks when she needed time to get herself together," he said, projecting his voice through the sudden silence. "Anyone is welcome, as long as they stay busy and sober. The facilities are clean and safe. Food's hot and good. The folks there will stand by you until you're ready to leave. Long afterward, too, if you let them." He pulled a battered stack of business cards from his wallet and offered them around.

One of the tough guys took one, then tossed it on the ground. A couple of others laughed, but took a card, too.

A small brown-haired woman covertly slid a card under the tattered cuff of her shirtsleeve.

He hoped that meant he might see her again.

"Let's go," Nicole whispered, offering a small, hip-high wave to the older woman.

And they hurried back to the SUV.

NICOLE'S HANDS SHOOK and her knees trembled as she buckled into the passenger seat of the SUV. She hadn't been anywhere near the industrial section of town since a detective had pulled her unconscious little sister off the ground in the middle of winter, high and barefoot. Being there again, with Cari missing, stole her breath and broke her heart.

Dean pressed the speaker button on his phone and dialed, then dropped the device into her cup holder before pulling onto the road. The word *Mama* appeared on the screen.

"Hello, baby boy." His mother's voice rose through the car, and Nicole's heart ached anew. She'd missed Mrs. Beaumont and Dean's entire family when they'd parted. She hadn't fully realized how much until now.

"Hey, Mama," Dean said, a broad smile curving his lips. "I've got you on speaker. I'm here with Nicole and Cari's little girl, Blakely."

"Hello, Nicole!" Mary Beaumont sang. "I've heard all about what's going on with Cari, and I'll tell you what I told Finn and Austin. Whatever trouble Cari's in, it's not her doing. Your sister's a good girl, and she left here with her head on straight. My boys will figure this out."

"Thank you," Nicole said. "I've really missed you, Mrs. Beaumont."

"Well, don't be a stranger. Come over. Let me get my hands on that niece of yours."

Nicole smiled, stealing a glance at Dean.

He bobbed his head, never one to say no to his mama.

"I will," Nicole said.

"Mama," Dean interrupted, making the final turn back onto Main Street. "I don't mean to rush you, but we're almost at our next stop. I called to tell you we were just down at the overpasses, and there's quite a few folks staying there again. I thought you could make sure they had something to eat tonight. I handed out a few cards. So you should probably know that, too."

"Good job," Mrs. Beaumont said. "I'll make up some sandwiches and send your dad down that way in a bit. I'll tell Lincoln to ride along."

Dean's brows rose and Nicole grinned.

The youngest Beaumont brother, Lincoln, had excelled in the military until he was captured during a mission that took the life of the younger soldier who'd gone with him. He'd returned home physically, but it'd been a long, slow process for him mentally and emotionally. Last she'd heard, he was doing okay, working as a ranch hand on the farm and not a fan of anyone or anything. Except maybe the young stables manager, Josie, but she was a whole lot of sunshine and he was a bit of a storm cloud.

Hopefully none of the tough guys they'd seen beneath the bridge gave him any trouble. Or back talk. Or sideways looks. They would unequivocally regret it.

"Now," Mrs. Beaumont said. "Nicole. How's your mama taking this? Is there anything I can do for her?"

"No, ma'am." Nicole cringed. "Mom's living in Charleston with my grandparents, and I haven't been able to reach her." It was one more thing on her growing pile of tasks and concerns.

"Has her number changed?" Mrs. Beaumont asked.

"No."

"That's settled then. I'll get a hold of your mama and invite her here to stay with me while this is sorted. How's that?"

Nicole's chest expanded with relief and gratitude. "I know she'd appreciate that."

Their mothers had become friends during the time Cari spent on the ranch, and the Beaumonts' property was large with numerous outbuildings turned guest rooms for anyone in need.

"Say no more," Mrs. Beaumont said.

"Thank you," Nicole repeated, meaning it to her core.

"All right, Mama," Dean cut in. "We'll swing by when we can. Love you."

"Love you, too, darlin'. See you soon, Nicole."

"Bye, Mrs. Beaumont," she called, missing the other woman, and her mother, so badly it hurt.

The call disconnected, and Nicole blew out a shaky breath. "I love your mama."

Dean slid her SUV into one of the spots on the street outside Ricky Rocket's Pizzas. "She loves you."

He climbed out and freed Blakely from her car seat, then met Nicole on the sidewalk and passed the baby her way.

She settled her niece into the sling and followed Dean into the pizza parlor, sending up silent prayers that Mikey would be there. And willing to talk.

The warm, rich scents of rising dough, stringy cheese and zesty sauce enveloped her as she crossed the threshold onto black-and-white-checkered flooring. Her stomach gurgled in response. A counter stretched across half of the back wall, leaving room for a small hallway on one side. Sets of round tables with chairs were scattered across the space, each with a metal napkin dispenser and shakers for Parmesan and pepper flakes.

A young woman in a Ricky Rocket's T-shirt and ball cap waited at the register. Her curly brown hair was thick and partially covered one eye. "Can I get something started for you?"

Dean made his way to her, full swagger activated.

Nicole followed, heart pounding.

"Hi," Dean said, resting a hip against the counter between them. "I'm Dean."

"Laney."

"Hi, Laney. I'm looking for Mikey. Any chance he's working today?"

Laney's gaze flickered to Nicole and Blakely.

Nicole tried to appear casual. "Mikey's a friend of my little sister."

The young woman's smile faltered, setting off alarm bells in Nicole's head. A quick look at Dean suggested he'd picked up on it as well.

"We were in the area and thought we'd stop by and see if we could catch him," Dean said, drawing her attention back to him.

"He's out right now. He's our only driver this shift, so he's just stopping in between deliveries to get the next bunch of orders."

Dean unleashed his full smile, and the girl's cheeks turned pink. "We'll wait," he said. "Can we get a couple of pepperoni strombolis in the meantime?"

"Sure."

Dean paid by credit card, then passed her some folded bills when he took his receipt. "Let me know when he gets back."

The young woman darted into the kitchen.

Nicole chose a table with full view of the front door and small hallway marked with signs for an office, restroom and exit. "I almost feel bad for her," she said, stroking Blakely's downy hair and clucking her tongue at Dean.

"Who?" He looked at the empty counter where the young woman had been. "Laney? Why?"

"You know why. You pull out that charming smile and lay on that sexy drawl and it confuses people. They probably never even know what's hit them."

"I was being polite, like my mama taught me," he countered. "I couldn't exactly come in here demanding to speak to Mikey. She wouldn't have wanted to help me."

"Oh." Nicole chuckled. "She definitely wants to help you."

Dean grinned and leaned his elbows on the table, crossing his arms before him. "Any chance you're speaking from experience?"

Nicole pursed her lips, fighting a silly smile. Her body and soul reacted to him the same way now as they had when they'd been together, even in the midst of a crisis. But she would never tell. "You drew me in with your quiet confidence at the ranch. My life and family were in chaos, and you had a profoundly peaceful vibe that I craved. The smile. The voice." The face and body... "The rest was just icing."

"And you think Laney liked the icing?" he asked, tipping his head to the register without breaking eye contact.

"Most folks do."

"What about you?" he asked.

"I've always been partial to the cake."

Dean barked a laugh, and Blakely jumped.

Nicole held her niece close, giggling softly into her curls.

It was just so easy to be comfortable with Dean. *Too easy*, she thought. And there was too much at stake for her to lose focus right now. She opened her mouth to change the subject, and the back door swung open.

A narrow figure strode inside and made an immediate turn away from view.

"Hey, Mikey," a deep male voice called in back. "Where ya been? You gotta move. We're backed up to Tuesday."

Dean was on his feet in a heartbeat, moving toward the counter.

Nicole stayed on his heels.

Workers were visible in the kitchen, preparing foods and hustling around the space.

Laney spoke to a guy with shaggy black hair, ripped jeans and a matching Ricky Rocket's T-shirt and hat. His Converse were tattered, and he had piercings in one eyebrow.

His face jerked in Nicole and Dean's direction, brow furrowing for one long beat before he broke into a run, scattering pizza boxes off the metal workstations in his wake.

"Hey!" the kitchen staff protested.

Mikey's shoes squeaked and slapped against the tiled floor a moment before the back door banged open, then shut.

Dean cussed under his breath, then looked at Nicole. "Go!"

He bolted down the hallway and through the back door, seconds behind Mikey.

Nicole pulled her phone from her pocket and hurried outside, eager to see the apprehension and notify Finn of the situation.

By the time she reached the rear lot, both men were gone.

Chapter Six

Nicole scanned the crumbling asphalt parking lot, the overflowing dumpster and handful of employee cars. The sedan with the delivery light on top was likely Mikey's, given that Laney said he was the only driver this shift. But if the car was still there, the two were clearly involved in a foot chase.

She stroked Blakely's hair and rocked gently back and forth, soothing her niece before she decided to fuss. It was nearing her next meal time, and Nicole had left her bag in the SUV, not expecting to be inside the pizzeria for more than a minute or two.

"Where did Uncle Dean go?" she whispered, straining her senses into the bright, sunny world.

Sounds of bleating tugboats and the rumbling of a distant train were all that could be heard, aside from the smooth crawl of tires over the street out front.

"I guess we'll wait inside," she told Blakely, tucking the cell phone away and turning back for the door. Dean would be back when he finished talking to Mikey, and if they were still running, she didn't want to interrupt. Mikey likely had the answers she needed. "First, we'll grab your bag and get your bottle ready. How does that sound?"

The strombolis Dean had ordered suddenly sounded like heaven. The toast and coffee she'd had at breakfast weren't nearly enough to get her through her day. And suddenly, she was famished.

She turned to tug the handle on the metal door behind them, but the door didn't budge. She braced her opposite arm around Blakely, careful not to jostle her, then tried again, harder this time. "Shoot."

Locked.

She blinked at a keypad above the knob. Employees probably had a code.

The sounds of footfalls turned her around once more. "Dean?"

The lot was empty.

Goose bumps raised the hairs along Nicole's arms and down the back of her neck. She moved to the edge of the building and wrapped her arms around Blakely on instinct, ready to make a run for the sidewalk out front.

A rough hand clamped over her mouth before she'd taken another step.

The man's large frame pressed against her back. His opposite arm curled over Blakely, crushing her against Nicole and causing her niece to scream in protest. The scent of something familiar and metallic, but unplaceable, sizzled in her rattled mind.

The sharp point of a blade pinched Nicole's side, and a whimper rattled up her windpipe. The cry was muffled against his unyielding palm. If she struggled, her attacker's weapon would win the battle. If either of them moved too much, or too suddenly, it would be Nicole who paid the price.

And if she fell, Blakely would fall with her.

A thousand horrifying thoughts raced through Nicole's mind. Was this what Cari had gone through? It couldn't be a coincidence that both sisters were in trouble only days apart.

Was she going to die without knowing her sister was okay?

The assailant's breath was hot against her cheek as he pressed his unshaven face against her temple. His mouth brushed her ear. "Stop looking for her," he whispered. His hold tightened, eliciting a primal scream from Blakely. "Understand?"

Nicole's eyes fell shut. She willed Dean to return to her. Or another employee to exit the rear door. For any kind of help at all. And above everything, someone to protect Blakely.

The knife pressed deeper, puncturing her shirt and tearing her skin.

She gasped as pain and panic flooded her system.

"Nod if you understand," he seethed.

She did as he asked, repeating the fervent, silent prayers for intervention.

"Good. Because the next time I come for you I'm taking your baby."

DEAN JOGGED BACK toward the pizzeria, eager to be with Nicole and Blakely again. A little embarrassed to say Mikey had gotten away. So much for being her superhero. Hopefully she wasn't worried when he didn't return immediately. He'd never dreamed a lanky man in worn-out Chucks could best him. Yet here he was.

He picked up his pace, surprised by the number of blocks he'd covered while lost in the chase. He could only hope, belatedly, that Nicole wouldn't see this as evidence of him choosing the job over her again.

He scrubbed a frustrated hand over his head, the hair hot from a beating sun. He hadn't caught Mikey, but the manager on duty might be willing to talk. Maybe he'd give up Mikey's contact information. Or perhaps the young woman from the register would. If not, Finn could get involved. Folks tended to comply when a badge showed up. His mind raced to piece together fresh backup plans for his backup plans so Nicole wouldn't feel more defeated than she already must.

The piercing scream of a baby broke his concentration and instinct jolted him into a run, his mind catching up a heartbeat later.

Blakely.

Sudden desperation moved him through the streets and alleys at fresh new speeds, warming his skin to combustion.

What was happening? Was it even Blakely who cried?

Every fiber of his being said yes. And he'd never heard her scream like that before.

He made the final cut through an alley and into Ricky Rocket's rear lot, then skidded to a stop.

A man had Nicole in his arms. His face pressed against her cheek from behind, dwarfing her narrow body. The assailant was at least half a foot taller than her and nearly doubly as broad. A dark hoodie pulled over his head hid his features, hair color and anything else Dean could attempt to use as identification.

Blakely's continuous screams wrenched Dean's gut.

"Freeze!" He shouted on instinct. His voice erupted in a deep, menacing growl. The words rumbled from his chest as he stalked forward, anger twisting in his veins. If this man so much as bruised either of them, Dean would make him live to regret it. "Let them go," he warned. "Now!"

Then Nicole was falling, shoved in a burst from the man's grip, and her attacker was bolting away.

Dean launched toward them, too far away to break their impact and terror-stricken by the possibility she wouldn't catch herself before hitting the ground.

"Nicole!"

Her knees collided with the pavement in a bone-jarring scrape. Her right palm slammed against the broken asphalt.

Blakely's scream was blood-chilling.

Dean slid across the ground to collect them, helping support Blakely's weight as Nicole lifted her torso, then collapsed onto her backside.

Tears streamed down her face as she stared at him and raised a palm for inspection, the skin covered in blood.

"I've got you," he cooed. "I'm right here. You're

okay. It's okay. I'm so sorry I left you. I won't do that again."

Nicole raised stunned eyes to him, then collapsed.

"Nicole!" Dean pulled Blakely from the sling and cradled her to his chest, then dug the phone from his pocket. "Shh," he soothed. "Shh."

The baby arched and screeched as he held her tight, struggling to dial his phone with trembling hands. He curled her against him, hating that he hadn't been there to protect her. Hating Nicole's still frame, despite her niece's distress.

Then he saw the blood on Blakely's clothes and the sling, still hooked over Nicole's head.

TWENTY MINUTES LATER, Nicole was awake inside an ambulance, being cared for by an EMT, and Blakely had devoured a bottle before going straight to sleep in Dean's arms.

His heart rate had barely slowed at all. The man who'd threatened Nicole had cut her, leaving a gash in her side. The wound had bled tremendously, but the responding EMT claimed it wasn't deep enough to necessitate stitches. Which was doubly good news since Nicole had made it clear she wasn't going to the hospital, where sutures were administered.

Instead, the EMT had cleaned and treated the area with glue and butterfly bandages. She'd apparently collapsed from stress and exhaustion; the shock of her assailant's shove had been her body's final straw.

Seeing Blakely soaked in blood and watching Nicole pass out was nearly Dean's unraveling. He wasn't sure he'd ever relax again.

Finn moved into view, stepping around a group of bystanders, being questioned about the man they'd witnessed running away from the scene of the attack. "How are you holding up?" he asked, stopping in front of Dean and Blakely.

Dean didn't have words for half of the things running circles in his head, so he stuck with the tried and true. "I'm okay. Did you get the jacket from the SUV?" He'd forgotten Cari's lavender jacket was in the back seat until he'd gone to retrieve Blakely's diaper bag. He should've delivered the evidence into Finn's hand the day before, but things had gotten out of control. Just as they had today.

"Already bagged and headed to forensics." Finn watched him closely, undoubtedly seeing more than Dean wanted to share. "This is a good look on you." He nodded to the sleeping baby in his brother's arms.

Dean glanced down as well. It wasn't a secret that he wanted a family of his own one day. Children he would keep and protect to his last breath. "Thanks. She's going through a lot. I can't imagine what her little mind is thinking. I hope she forgets as much of this as possible."

Finn shifted, offering a small smile. "If it helps, I don't know anyone who remembers anything from this age."

"It helps."

"How's Nicole doing?"

Dean's gaze moved to the open ambulance doors

where Nicole spoke with the EMT. "He's forcing an IV of fluid on her, hopefully with something mild for pain. No stitches, as long as she takes it easy."

Finn snorted. "Good luck with that."

Dean swallowed a groan. "Yeah. Thanks."

Nicole's sister was missing, and the man who'd just knifed her admitted to knowing something about the situation.

Nicole would very likely need the stitches soon.

He ran a palm down his face, then tipped his head toward the remaining bystanders. "Were you able to get a good description?"

Finn's expression said the answer was no. "We've got a good start," he hedged. "More than a dozen people saw a man in a dark hoodie running from this direction. Only about three of them had details beyond that, but those all matched, so it's something."

"He was tall," Dean said, recalling the horrific scene with perfect detail. "At least my height. And broad. Her shoulders were completely concealed by him. I could only see her legs and hear Blakely's screams."

Finn dropped his gaze to the baby once more. "Did the EMT take a look at her?"

"Yeah. Nicole refused treatment until Blakely had been evaluated. Any new leads on Cari?"

"Aside from this guy?" Finn asked. "No. But Nicole says he didn't know Blakely was Cari's kid. He referred to her as Nicole's child. So he doesn't know Cari personally. That goes along with what we expected. Whatever she's gotten wrapped up in isn't about her. I'm not sure how much Mikey could've helped, even if you'd caught him."

Dean narrowed his eyes. "Thanks for reminding me of that."

Finn laughed. "Hey, what are little brothers for?"

"Finn?" Nicole's voice drew their attention to where she crouched at the edge of the ambulance bay, one hand pressed to her newly bandaged side. "A little help?"

Finn obliged.

Dean followed him, watching carefully as his brother helped her down.

Her body language and facial expression suggested significant pain and discomfort. Given the way things could've gone today, Dean chose to be thankful.

He also told himself she'd asked Finn, instead of him, for help because Blakely was asleep in his arms, and she didn't want to risk waking her. But he couldn't help wondering if Nicole was upset with him for leaving her unprotected.

"We can go," she said.

The EMT frowned as he peeled protective gloves from his hands. "If you don't want to go to the hospital for stitches, you're going to have to rest and be still so your body can do the work." He shot pointed looks at Dean and Finn, then fixed her with a hard stare. "I mean it. No overexertion. Change the bandage regularly and go to the ER if you have any of the symptoms we talked about."

She responded with a polite but dismissive smile. "Thank you."

She looked longingly at Blakely, but didn't ask to hold her. "All right. What did we learn?" she asked, bouncing her attention from one Beaumont to the other.

"We're working on it," Finn said. "Folks on the sidewalk reported a guy roughly our size—" he motioned from himself to Dean "—wearing a dark hoodie, sneakers and jeans. Possibly with shaggy brown hair."

Nicole visibly deflated. "After all this, we don't even have a thorough description?"

Finn looked a bit sheepish, though he'd done all he could do. "We're pulling security video from shops on the block. I'll keep you in the loop as new details come to light."

She hugged herself and nodded. "He was heavier than the two of you, less…fit. His breaths were rough instead of even, and I could feel his middle pressed against me. He was soft, not—" Her cheeks darkened.

Finn grinned. "Fit? Like me?"

Dean frowned.

"Yeah." Nicole laughed softly, then winced, presumably at a jolt of pain.

"Assailant with a dad bod," Finn said. "That helps. Anything else?"

"Maybe. He smelled like something vaguely familiar, but I haven't decided what yet. In the moment, I was too panicked. Right now, my mind feels a little warped. I'll let you know when it comes to me."

Finn nodded. "Sounds like a plan."

The pizzeria's back door opened, and a man in

a white T-shirt and apron appeared with a piece of paper in hand. "Detective Beaumont?"

"Right here." Finn moved across the lot to accept the paper.

The man retreated inside.

"What's that?" Nicole asked, taking the words out of Dean's mouth.

Finn smiled. "Mike Litchfield's contact information and work schedule for the next two weeks."

Nicole's expression brightened. "That's good. Do you think he'll go home? Or hide out? Will he even come back here after Dean chased him?"

"We'll know soon enough," Finn said. "I'll get a man outside his home and the pizzeria. The manager knows to contact me if he hears from Mikey."

"Any word on the black sedan?" Dean asked.

"Not yet, but I'll be in touch if that changes." He stepped away with one hand raised in goodbye. "I've got to get back to it, but y'all take care and keep in touch. Rest, Nicole."

She sighed but didn't protest.

Instead, she slid an arm around Dean's back and let him curl her against him in a gentle embrace, while Blakely snored softly between them.

Chapter Seven

Nicole changed into yoga pants and an oversize T-shirt when they returned to her apartment. Excess adrenaline poured through her, trembling her limbs and rattling her thoughts. Was this day even real? It didn't seem possible, and yet she would surely have a scar to prove it.

She could only pray Cari wasn't faring any worse.

It only took a minute for Nicole to choose her bed over the couch for rest, even as Dean tucked Blakely into her crib, then went to make tea. She slid beneath the cool covers, then pulled the fabric up to meet her chin. She'd thought the night Cari didn't come home from work was the worst of her life. Then last night, when she still hadn't come home, and Nicole had been chased by a black sedan twice, she'd been sure that was as bad as it could get. This morning, when she'd had to face the awful reality of the industrial park and confront the internal demons from her past, she'd never guessed that would be the easiest part of her day. Never dreamed she'd be held at knifepoint. And stabbed. The idea was inconceivable. And terrifying. Blakely had been right there in her arms.

A tear slid over her cheek and onto the pillow where she'd rested her head, knees curled up to her chest. The sting in her bandaged side grew, and she longed for sleep. But guilt and worries crept in. Blakely would wake again soon, and Nicole couldn't keep asking Dean for help. It was Nicole's responsibility to care for her niece. And she was failing.

She had naively believed she could protect her sister, too.

She closed her eyes tight and willed an untapped sisterly instinct to manifest and reveal Cari's location. Instead, her attacker's unshaven face and sticky breath on her skin came back with a crash. Her eyes opened, and her gut coiled. That man knew where Cari was. He knew what was happening to her. The answers Nicole needed had been so close, and now they were gone.

A gentle rap against the doorjamb drew Nicole's attention.

Dean stood in the hallway with a tray. "Sorry. I knocked lightly to see if you were asleep."

"I'm not." She wiped her tears discreetly and scooted upward on the mattress, rearranging her pillows to support her back against the headboard. The scents of her favorite comfort foods made her stomach shout with glee. "Is that for me?"

"Chicken noodle soup and grilled cheese." He carried the tray into her room and lowered it onto the nightstand. "You only had toast at breakfast. I thought you might be hungry. I also brought water. And these." He opened his palm to reveal a pair of over-the-counter painkillers.

Nicole took the pills and opened the bottle of water. "Thank you. Are you eating?"

"I will. I wanted to check on you first. It's not exactly Ricky Rocket's stromboli, but…"

"It's better," she said, carefully moving the tray onto her lap. She swallowed the painkillers, then lifted one of the sandwich triangles in Dean's direction. "Sit. Share with me."

He accepted, reluctantly taking a seat at the edge of her bed. "When I chased Mikey, I wasn't choosing work over you and Blakely," he said, looking strangely pained.

She frowned. "I didn't think that." She reached for him on instinct, curling her free hand over his. "Not for a second. And I don't blame you for what happened to me today, in case that's where this is going. I wanted you to chase Mikey. I think he could know something useful. I blame myself for following you outside. In my mind, I was going to find the two of you arguing in the lot. Even though we were followed twice yesterday, it never occurred to me that we might be followed again today."

"I looked for it," Dean said. "The black sedan. When we were in the SUV, I was watching. When we were talking to the folks at the underpasses, I was watching. Once we parked on Main Street, my focus changed, and I should know better. It's my job to be vigilant and cautious."

Nicole bit into her half of the sandwich, unsure anything they could've done differently would've mattered. Aside from giving up the search for Cari, and that wasn't happening. "This isn't the same as your other jobs," she said. "You usually work alone, or with your brothers who are trained to handle those situations. I'm sure they could've defended themselves."

"They all carry weapons, not babies," he said, remorse still etched across his face. "I'm not sure what anyone could've done in your shoes."

"Still," she said. The Beaumont men were tall and lean. They'd grown up working the land and helping with the ranch. She'd called them fit earlier, but that didn't begin to describe their sheer muscle and utter capability. They'd all spent time in the military, been trained to remain calm and handle any type of pressure. Not to mention their hand-to-hand combat skills were action film-worthy. Watching them spar for fun had always been Nicole's guilty pleasure when she and Dean were together. Frankly, she wouldn't say no to watching a match now, either. "I shouldn't have let myself get into that situation," she said. "It won't happen again."

Dean didn't push. He stroked his thumb along her fingers and took a bite of his sandwich.

It had always been moments like these that turned her to putty for Dean Beaumont. The cups of tea and grilled cheese sandwiches. The way he listened when she spoke and remembered the things she said. He treated everyone as if they were his top priority, and he treated her as if she mattered most in the world.

Nicole could be vulnerable with Dean. She could be anything with Dean.

He polished off his half of the sandwich and grinned. "Not bad."

She agreed. Something about the moment felt hopeful. "I wish I could tell Cari how hard we're working," she said. "If she knew we were all out here looking, that Blakely is okay, and your mama is inviting our mom to stay at the ranch until Cari's home... I think that would give her hope." Nicole pressed her lips tight. "I wish she knew we were coming."

"She knows," Dean said, his low, confident voice making it impossible not to believe.

"Yeah?"

"Nicole." His expression caught somewhere between sincerity and disbelief. "Everyone who's ever met you knows you would move mountains for your sister. She does, too. And she's going to keep fighting until you get there, because Homes women don't quit."

Nicole's throat tightened, and she wiped her face with a napkin from the tray. "Sorry. I can't seem to stick with one emotion for more than five minutes."

"Extreme exhaustion and a recent stabbing will do that." Dean deadpanned.

She laughed. "See? Ow." She pressed a palm to her burning wound. "Stop."

He raised his hand in innocence, but mischief twinkled in his eyes. "All right. I'll leave you to finish your soup. Drink the water. Later, we'll think of something we can do from the apartment to generate a new lead."

"Deal." She dipped a spoon into the soup, watching with regret as he moved back through her door. She gave silent gratitude for every bite of a meal she didn't have to make, and for each minute Blakely continued to rest.

When the bowl was empty and her half sandwich gone, she returned the tray to the nightstand and scooted under the blankets. Then she closed her eyes.

When Blakely's laughter roused her sometime later, Nicole was surprised to learn nearly two hours had passed. Her side was tender as she moved to sit up, but the pain she'd felt earlier was significantly dulled.

Dean's rumbling chuckle brought a smile to her lips, and she swung her legs over the edge of the bed.

A few moments later, her niece and her hero came into view on the living room floor. Blakely wore a black bodysuit and rainbow-colored tutu. The short hair at the top of her head was arranged into two tiny pigtails that looked a little like antennae.

Blakely erupted in giddy screeches as her pony-shaped teether galloped over her round tummy, powered by the handsome sitter at her side.

Dean made clip-clopping hoof sounds, then laughed again when Blakely couldn't seem to stop.

The scene gripped Nicole's heart. Want, regret and a whole host of other emotions she wasn't ready to unpack rose to the surface. But she pressed them all back down.

"Hey," Dean said, crunching effortlessly into a sit. "How'd you sleep? Better than last night?"

"Much." She moved in his direction, catching her niece's eye. "Thank you again."

Blakely made spit bubbles and kicked her chubby, dimpled legs, vocalizing her joy at her favorite aunt's appearance.

Dean scooped her off the floor and stood before Nicole could bend to lift her. "I've got her," he said. "No need to dead lift this chunk when I'm a perfectly good delivery option." He passed her yammering niece into her arms.

Nicole pulled her in close and nuzzled her warm soft skin. "I love you so much," she whispered, dotting Blakely's face and hair with kisses. "You have no idea."

"Maybe you should sit," Dean suggested.

"No time," Nicole said. "Right, Blakely?" She turned back toward the hallway with a fresh idea in her rested mind. "I think we should message Mikey again. This time we need to come clean. Let him know it was us at the pizzeria and why we were there. Otherwise, who knows what he thinks is happening. He might avoid his home and the pizza shop if he's in some kind of trouble and thinks you're after him."

Dean's soft footfalls moved down the hall behind her, never missing a beat. "It can't hurt. We've given him plenty of time to respond to our last message, and he hasn't."

"Exactly what I was thinking. And if he cares about Cari at all, and isn't part of the reason she's gone, he should want to help us." Nicole sat at the small computer desk in her sister's room and balanced Blakely on her legs.

She set one hand on the keys, but the words didn't come.

Dean moved to her side. He placed a palm on her shoulder, offering his silent strength.

"You're right," she said, grabbing on to the unspoken encouragement. "I just need to do it." She blew out a breath and began typing. "Hi Mikey," she spoke the words as she typed. "I'm Cari's sister, Nicole. Maybe you've heard of me."

The story unfolded as she pecked, one-handed, at the keyboard, cradling Blakely with her other arm. Within minutes, Nicole had outlined her last two days and added a plea for help. "Anything you might know about what she's been up to, or who she's been with, anything at all might make the difference between finding her in time or after it's too late. Please. Please help me."

Blakely slapped a drool-covered hand against her aunt's chest and squealed with delight.

Nicole stifled a desperate scream. How had all her hope landed in the hands of a pizza guy who ran when anyone asked for him? "I hope that enthusiasm means you think this message was perfect, Blakely."

Dean dropped into a squat beside her chair. "I think our little ninja ballerina is right."

"Is that what you've dressed her as?" Nicole asked, swinging her face toward his. She'd assumed the look was unintentional, a result of Dean pulling wardrobe pieces from Blakely's drawers at random.

He glanced her way, brow furrowed. "Well, yeah. But look."

She followed his gaze to the screen.

Three tiny dots bounced beneath her message. Mikey was typing.

Nicole reminded herself to breathe.

Then the dots stopped.

"What happened?" she asked, looking frantically from the screen to Dean and back. "Where'd the dots go? Why'd they stop?"

Before Dean could answer, Cari's laptop emitted the sudden peppy bing-bong sound announcing an incoming video call.

"He's calling," she whispered. "What do I do?"

Dean reached for the device and accepted the call.

Mikey wore a beanie over his shaggy dark hair, despite the heat. He chewed the skin along the sides of his fingernails, gaze darting as he moved along an empty sidewalk.

"Hi," Nicole said. "Thank you so much for calling. I didn't know who else to ask for help. You've known her for years, and I'm just hoping—"

"Stop," he said, eyes snapping back to the camera. "Stop. I don't know what's going on with your sister. I can't help you."

Nicole's hopeful heart crashed. "But—"

"Listen lady, I said I don't know. And I don't."

Dean turned the laptop in his direction by a half inch, bringing him into the frame. "I'm Dean Beaumont. I'm a private investigator and personal friend of Cari's and Nicole's. You should know a man held Nicole and Cari's baby at knifepoint today. He stabbed her when I got back from chasing after you, so this is serious, and you need to treat it that way."

Mikey stilled, and his gaze jumped to Nicole. "Seriously?"

She nodded, holding Blakely closer and fighting the surge of mixed emotion. "Please help us."

Mikey cursed. He rubbed his cheek, then scratched his head, fidgeting and shifting his weight as he paused outside a boarded-up garage. "I want to help, but look, I'm not the hero to your story. I'm not the hero in any story."

"Mikey," Dean cut in. "My brother is the detective assigned to Cari's disappearance," he said. "He's good at what he does, and so am I. So is my partner. Anything you can tell us has the potential to help save your friend's life."

Mikey debated a long moment, then caved. "Fine. I'm the one who helped Cari get the party gigs, but I didn't talk to her last night. And none of the servers have to do anything they don't want to do."

Nicole's gut twisted instantly, fear and nausea fought for position with her anger. "What does that mean?"

He crunched his features into a look of disbelief, as if she were the one saying ridiculous things. "It means the jobs pay well for a reason. Servers take the money and keep quiet about what they see or hear. If they ever want in on a chance to make more, those opportunities are there, too."

Nicole couldn't bring herself to ask the next, most obvious, question.

Dean's fingers curled into fists on the desktop, and he pulled them onto his lap. "Did Cari ever take on any of the extra opportunities?"

Mikey's expression turned instantly to offense. "Hell no. Man, I thought you said you knew her." He swung his attention back to Nicole, as she sank against the chair with relief. "Cari was always cautious, and she was saving money. She never said why. Baby stuff, I guess."

"She applied to colleges," Nicole said, pride thick in her voice. "She was trying to make a better life for her and Blakely."

Mikey bobbed his head. "Yeah, that sounds like her. It's why I told her about the special gigs. But I can't talk to you anymore. Either of you," he said, shooting pointed looks at Dean, then back. "So stop looking for me, and stop messaging me, because I don't have anything else to say. If something bad is going down, then you guys have already put a target on my back by coming to work and chasing me around. I've got enough problems. You know what I'm saying? Anyone who didn't know I had a connection to a missing girl, or these gigs, probably does now. And that's no good for anyone. So I'm out. Stop coming for me or I'll be next."

"Who's your contact for the parties?" Dean asked. "How can I get in touch with them?"

Mikey shook his head, flashed a peace sign and disconnected the call.

A moment later, the app showed he'd signed off.

Mikey was gone.

Chapter Eight

Dean returned to the living room, giving Nicole the space she requested after the call with Mikey. The video chat had only lasted a few minutes, but there had been plenty to process. Like the fact that Mikey was clearly scared, which didn't bode well for Cari. Mikey was mixed up in something dangerous and probably illegal. He hadn't been specific, but the implications he'd made were enough.

Dean dialed Finn to fill him in on the new information, but the call landed in voice mail. He sent a text instead of leaving a message, asking him to get in touch.

His next text went to Austin. As private investigators, Austin and Dean had a handful of informants and a whole lot of experience navigating the unsavory groups in town. If Cari's disappearance wasn't a random kidnapping or carjacking, the PIs' connections would go just as far as the long arm of the law.

The message was barely marked as delivered before Austin's response returned.

Austin: omw

On my way.

Dean blew out a breath of relief and poured a glass of water. Sitting on the sidelines when something needed done wasn't his style, but someone had to be there for Nicole, and he couldn't think of anyone else he'd want to take his stead.

She appeared with Blakely a long while later. Her hair had been swept into a ponytail, and her smile was an obvious ruse, likely meant for her niece. The hope he'd seen in her eyes before speaking with Mikey was long gone. "My mom called."

"Yeah?" Dean asked, mildly glad to know she hadn't simply been avoiding him all this time. Still, his muscles bunched with tension. Every polite follow-up that came to mind was ridiculous. *How's she doing? How'd it go? Are you okay?* Those answers were so obvious, he couldn't bring himself to speak the words. Instead, he did his best to appear calm and casual, encouraging her to elaborate when she was ready.

"My grandpa had a medical scare yesterday. Mom spent the day at the hospital while they ran a gamut of tests and kept him for observation. She got my message, but I didn't tell her what was going on, so she waited to call until she got some sleep. Grandpa's home now, and Grandma made an appointment for him to see a specialist next week."

"He's okay?" Dean asked.

"Mom thinks so, but she'll know more after the next appointment. Meanwhile, she's on her way here. Your mama left a message for her, too. I told her to give Mrs. Beaumont a call when we hung up. She's going to take her up on the offer to stay at the ranch for a while. A neighbor is going to check in on my grandparents and make sure Grandpa gets to his next appointment if Mom's not back in time." Nicole bounced Blakely gently as she rocked foot to foot. "Mom's having a hard time."

"Being here will help," Dean said, wondering just how awful it must feel for Mrs. Homes to know her aging parents needed her, but so did her daughters, and she couldn't be in two different states at once.

He longed to reach for Nicole. He ached to comfort her. But he wasn't sure how to do that without overstepping. Caring for Blakely, making sure Nicole rested and was fed, that was easy. That didn't involve getting into her space. Suddenly, the shared history that'd made it so easy to drop everything and help her felt like an impossible divide.

They'd been in love once, and they'd hurt each other badly. He'd been a terrible boyfriend, retreated inward when he couldn't deal with the loss of Ben Smothers, the eight-year-old boy he didn't find in time to save. After seeing the way Nicole had stuck by her sister, he'd wrongly assumed she'd stay through his crisis, too. But she'd walked out on Dean at his lowest point. She'd drawn a line for him. And he hadn't fought to keep her. She'd done what she had to do to protect herself, but it'd felt like abandonment in the moment nonetheless.

He'd let her leave, but he'd never really let her go. He wanted her in his arms and in his life again, right now. Same as always. He wanted Nicole in a real and long-term way, but there was a mountain of old wounds between them. And right now, all that mattered was finding Cari.

Nicole made a bottle for Blakely, then carried both into the living room, sharp eyes fixed on him. "You okay?"

"Yeah, sorry." He forced his thoughts to the moment at hand.

Her head tilted slightly over one shoulder, and her eyes narrowed.

A knock at the door saved Dean from a conversation he wasn't ready to have.

He hurried in the direction of the sound. "That's probably Austin," he said, pausing to check the peephole before letting his brother inside.

"Hey." Austin greeted Dean with a loose one-armed hug. "How y'all holding up?"

Dean nodded in answer to the inane question then locked the door while Austin greeted Nicole and Blakely.

"Has there been any news?" Nicole asked, a cautious thread of hope in her tone.

Austin's polite expression faltered. "I'm just here touching base."

"I thought we should fill one another in on what we know," Dean said.

Austin slowly extricated the baby from Nicole's arms. "Your auntie isn't supposed to exert herself, so I'm going to sneak in here and make you love me best."

He turned to Dean with a wink.

Nicole rolled her eyes but didn't argue. "I'll put on the coffee."

Within minutes, they'd settled around the small kitchen table, floral-patterned mugs in hand. Nicole reported on the details of her attack and the conversation with Mikey, answering Austin's questions as they came. Dean did his best to maintain his cool facade, though both stories made him want to run his fist through a virtual stranger.

"How about you?" he asked his brother, when the volleys between Austin and Nicole had gone silent.

Austin cleared his throat, the only sign so far that Nicole's awful day had affected him, too. "I spent a little time with Finn at the station," he said. "He's got a plan in motion, but he's shorthanded, so I'm helping with legwork. Small towns, small police departments," he explained to Nicole, though she'd spent enough time with his family to fully understand.

"Tell me more about the plan," she prompted.

Austin shifted, shaking a rattle at Blakely, safely strapped into the high chair at his side. "Tech support is pinging Cari's phone. It hasn't been on, so there's no signal, but they're looking. The next time it's powered up, they'll be able to track it."

Dean turned his mug between his palms, fighting the creeping feeling of failure. "I think we need to track down Mikey. He was scared, and I think he's in trouble. He was convinced Nicole and I had caused him real problems by showing up at the pizzeria. I don't want that to be true. I'm hoping our folks will intervene, give him refuge and a chance to change his trajectory in life, if you can find him."

"I'll see what I can do," Austin said. "Finn's got a cruiser watching the guy's house and Ricky Rocket's. I'll ask around downtown, see if anyone knows him. Maybe talk to the staff in some local shops, the record store, bookstore, skate shop. Someone's seen him, or seen him with someone they know. I'll follow the bread crumbs until I've got him."

"Let's hope you're faster than whoever he thinks is after him."

Nicole pulled her hair from its tie, finger-combing it as she listened, then put it up again. She dragged her gaze from one brother to the other. "What do you think Mikey meant when he said the waitstaff had opportunities to make more money if they wanted? Was he talking about..." She tensed, expression flat. "Prostitution? Drugs? Something else? Something worse?"

Dean's hand drifted in her direction, intending to cover and squeeze her trembling fingers, but their eyes met and he withdrew.

Austin's eyebrow ticked. Of course his brother had noticed.

That was the problem with belonging to a family of investigators. They saw everything. And if what they saw was even remotely related to romance, their mama would know inside the hour. Sometimes they didn't even have to report it to her. She just knew.

"We'll have answers when we catch up to Mikey," Austin said. "Speculation will only distract us and waste time. Better to get the facts from the source. What did you notice in the background during the call? Any idea where he was?"

"He kept the camera close, but he seemed to be on an empty sidewalk somewhere," Dean said. "No passing cars. No shoppers. Not downtown. I didn't hear the tugboats or see water either, so probably not near the docks."

"What about traffic sounds? Could he have been near the overpasses?"

"No." Dean imagined the area his brother mentioned, and another thought came to mind. "I asked Mama to get some food out that way tonight. Any chance you've talked to her? There were quite a few folks down there who looked like they could use a meal. She mentioned sending Dad and Lincoln."

Austin's lips twisted into a wry smile. "Lincoln told me all about it."

Nicole tensed. "Is everything okay?"

"Dad stood him up," Austin said. "Then the next thing Lincoln knew, Josie's on her way to the truck with Mama's sandwiches."

"No," Nicole whispered, delight lifting her features. She leaned over her mug, awaiting details.

Dean snorted. He'd forgotten how invested she'd always been in the unlikely pairing. It was no wonder Nicole and his mother got along so well.

Lincoln and Josie had some sort of connection that neither of them talked about and both refused to act on, as far as anyone knew. Dean suspected a big part of the reason was his brother. It'd taken three years for

Lincoln to come back to himself after the things he'd endured as a soldier. He was darker now, more withdrawn and cautious. Except when it came to Josie.

Josie was several years younger than Lincoln. Their folks had taken her in when she was a teen struggling with a series of bad choices and no support system. Lincoln had been in the military at the time and only met Josie when he was home on leave, but the Beaumonts suspected part of Lincoln still thought of Josie as a kid, or worse, as kin. If they were right, it was easy to see why he'd struggle with the obvious attraction. Mama assumed Lincoln was letting Josie set the pace, and their dad said Lincoln was taming his own demons before letting anyone else get close enough to be hurt by them.

Whatever the reason, the slow burn had been killing the lot of them for years.

"Cops are still pulling security footage from shops near Ricky Rocket's," Austin said. "So far the images of the assailant are too distant and pixelated to make a solid identification. Finn's asked the tech lab to look for signs of the black sedan that followed you as well. If we can't get an ID on the man, maybe we can get a plate on the car he's driving."

"Assuming it's his car," Dean said.

Austin clasped his hands on the table, shooting Dean a bland expression. "No matter whose it is, the car's a lead." He turned back to Nicole. "Even if the car was stolen, it's a lead. We can look at who it was taken from and where, then scope out that person and their location. Things don't happen in a vacuum. There's always a witness or loose end. We just have to find it and pull. Any chance you got a screenshot of Mikey's face?"

"No," Nicole answered. "But I saw photos of him on Cari's computer. I can get those for you if you want."

"I'd appreciate it," he said. "Text them to me and Finn when you get time. Also, send any social media handles you have for him. Dean told me about the Mikey Likey account, so I'll do a deep dive on that later, see who his contacts are, where he frequents and who he's in photos with. I'll look into the friends' accounts, too. See if I can find any connection to a catering service or restaurant, other than Ricky Rocket's. Finn's already interviewed everyone there. I'll also look for a connection between Mikey's online acquaintances and the homeowners at the address where Cari last worked."

Dean rubbed the backs of his fingers along his unshaven cheeks. "Sounds like a plan."

Austin fought a smile, eyeballing Dean's unusually scruffy face. "It's something. You growing a beard or what?"

"I need to get home and pick up some things. My truck, too. I didn't expect to be gone for the night when I left yesterday."

"I've got a go bag in the truck, if you want it." His gaze flickered to Nicole, then Blakely. "It'll set you up for two or three days if you're not ready to make the run home."

Dean sighed in relief. He hadn't wanted to go back

out today, but he was in need of a shower and fresh clothes. "Thanks. I'll take it."

Austin rose and carried his mug to the sink. "Thank you for the coffee and company, Nicole." He patted her shoulder playfully on his way to the high chair, where he blew raspberries against Blakely's neck.

She erupted into laughter that spread through the adults in the room.

"Hold on." Nicole rose and wrapped her arms around Austin's middle, flinching slightly with the movement. "I've missed you. And I really appreciate all you're doing for my family."

"Anything. Anytime." Austin pulled back and looked into her eyes. "We're going to find Cari and bring her home. Now go sit yourself down and get your feet up. You were stabbed today."

Dean's gut twisted at the scene, the sweet familiarity between them, and longing for what might've been.

Nicole went to the couch and made a show of putting both feet up.

Austin grinned. "I'll be right back."

Dean lifted Blakely from her high chair and waited for his brother to return with the bag.

He reappeared a moment later. "Keep me posted if you hear anything new or have something else I can grab on to."

"Count on it."

Chapter Nine

Dean woke with the sun and an aching back the next morning. Nicole's living room was not suited for sleep. No wonder she hadn't felt rested the night before, stress and anxiety aside. He'd felt better after three hours on her recliner than following an entire night on the sofa.

He arched his back and rolled his shoulders, working out the knotted muscles as he paced her living room.

Nicole had fallen asleep shortly after Blakely, a testament to her pain and fatigue. She'd surprised him with her willingness to take more over-the-counter medication after changing her bandage and calling it a night.

If he had to hazard a guess, he'd say her reasons for taking such good care of herself had more to do with healing quickly for Blakely's sake than her own. But the reason didn't matter. He was just glad not to have to fight her on the pills and rest.

Dean toted Austin's blessed go bag to the bathroom and rushed through his usual morning routine. Showered, shaved and dressed in a navy blue T-shirt and jeans, he was ready for a whole lot of black coffee.

Blakely rose before he'd poured his second mug, and he nabbed her from her crib before she got too wound up.

He'd wisely moved the baby monitor's speaker from Nicole's room the night before so she wouldn't be disturbed this morning. He'd left the device in the kitchen while he brewed coffee.

He made a mental note to thank his mama for letting him and his brothers help out with babies and toddlers over the years. He'd been calling on that experience and training more every day since Nicole and her niece had arrived at his place. *Keep 'em fed, clean and dry* were his mama's words of wisdom when he'd struggled to make his foster brothers and sisters happy. Her follow-up advice had always been, *hold 'em and entertain them. If none of that works, call Mama.*

Thankfully a dry diaper and full bottle had pleased Blakely. From there, he'd taken her to the room she shared with Cari. "Time to get you out of these goofy pajamas," he suggested, peering into the closet of pint-sized clothes. Her black-and-white ensemble was hilarious but unfortunate. "You look like you just busted out of an old-timey jail," he said. "What is your auntie doing to you?"

Dean selected a red plaid sundress and socks that looked like cowgirl boots, then rested her on the changing table. "Did you know everyone I love is out there looking for your mama right now? No one's going to give up until she's back here with you. They're all very good at their jobs, even if one or two of them look too young or as if they aren't paying attention. Then again, there probably aren't a lot of people who look young to you."

He tugged the dress over her head and the socks onto her feet. "I'm hoping to stay here and help your auntie while she heals. She loves you and your mama very much, and this is a tough time for her. Don't tell her I told you this," he said, stretching a springy head-band with a big fake flower over her wispy brown curls and arranging the flower near one ear. "But she's very important to me. Has been for a long while, and I can't imagine that ever changing. I can prom-ise you I won't let anything bad happen to her again. She's stubborn, so she won't like knowing I'm look-ing out for her too closely. Which means I'm trusting you to keep this intel on the DL. That's the down-low. We'll learn more PI terms after breakfast."

Blakely cooed and babbled as he curled her against his chest and headed back down the hallway, past a closed bedroom door.

His footfalls slowed when Nicole came into view at the kitchen table, a mug of coffee poised at her lips. The baby monitor glowing merrily on the coun-ter at her side.

He willed his expression to remain unmoved, told himself she somehow hadn't overheard his conversa-tion through the speaker sitting three feet away and hoped he hadn't just added more stress to her life. "Morning."

"Morning," she said. The slight curve at the corner of her mouth suggested she'd heard every word and maybe wasn't mad about it. "Were you able to sleep?"

"A little. You?"

"Mmm-hmm. I just took a couple more pain pills with water and helped myself to coffee. Feel like joining me for a bagel?"

"Sure." He put Blakely into her playpen and started the mobile of tiny hedgehogs for her entertainment.

Nicole pushed two bagels into the toaster. "Great. After this, I thought we could go for a drive."

NICOLE STRETCHED HER arm through the open window on the passenger side of her SUV. Dean had graciously agreed to drive her and Blakely around again, which was good, because Nicole had never been good at staying inside for long periods of time. Walking or jogging in the fresh air was her go-to method for processing emotions. She'd experienced more turmoil in the last few days than in the past year, and she wasn't in any condition or position to go out alone.

The wound on her side was trying to heal, and the area was tender, sensitive to movement. Changing the bandage had revealed the glue and tape were working their magic. Still, going anywhere alone seemed unwise. And she'd likely feel the larger effects of her attack long after a permanent scar had formed. The follow-up appointment she truly needed was with a licensed trauma counselor, not an MD.

Nicole opened and closed her hand against the beating wind as Dean drove along the coast. Her favorite summertime playlist rose from the speakers on shuffle. She did her best to soak up the sun and find peace in the moment, but it proved an impossible task.

She was outside, but she wasn't walking or running or pushing away her cares. She was in a car with a man whose entire family was helping her find her missing sister. And no part of her could forget that for a millisecond.

"Maybe we should visit the people who helped us find Mikey before," she said. "They might know more now, or there could be someone new." She stared at Dean's freshly shaven cheek, aching to stroke it with her fingertips and turn him to face her. "Please?"

Dean cast a wary glance in her direction, then made the next available turn.

She smiled, and her shoulders sagged with relief. "Thank you."

"I thought about that group all night, wondering what kind of impression Lincoln made. I'm hoping the food and added interaction built some more trust. I know it's not too late for any of them to turn things around, and I know my folks can help."

Nicole watched intently as the scenery changed, anxiety rapidly climbing over her. Just as it had the day before, and as it always would when visiting this particular part of town.

She straightened when the overpasses came into view, the space unchanged, the view drastically different. "What's going on?" she asked, pulling her sunglasses from her eyes. "Where'd they all go?"

Dean stopped in the middle of the desolate street,

in the shadow of an overarching highway system. Twenty-four hours prior, there had been a dozen people lingering there, along with makeshift tents and other evidence at least a few had called this place their home. Now there was only scattered debris and silence.

"I don't know." He eased the SUV forward, eyes clinging to the emptiness.

"Were they here when Lincoln and Josie brought sandwiches?"

"I think Lincoln would've called if they weren't," Dean said, returning his eyes to the road. His tone and expression were the perfect picture of calm, but there was tension in his jaw and grip on her steering wheel.

Dean was clearly as startled as she was. He was just better at hiding it.

She'd always envied that. Her emotions were written in neon across her face and heart, hanging perpetually from her sleeve.

"Do you think something bad happened to them?" she asked.

Mikey had been afraid when they chatted last night. He thought she and Dean had put him in danger by looking for him. What did that mean for a group of people they'd actually had the chance to speak with?

"I don't know."

Nicole's mind raced with awful possibilities. "Can we drive by the house where Cari worked?"

He cast another cautious glance in her direction. "Why?"

"I don't know. I guess because it's the last place

she was supposed to be. What if I missed something before?"

Dean nodded, apparently lost in thought.

Behind them, in her rear-facing car seat, Blakely made enthusiastic baby sounds, kicking her dimpled baby feet into view.

"She's happy," Dean noted, catching Nicole's eyes as she turned back to face the windshield. "I guess she likes the car?"

"I'm not sure what's going on with her. She doesn't mind the car, but she's usually asleep by now," Nicole said. It was nice that her niece wasn't upset about being stuck in her car seat for another extended ride, but she suspected the contentment wouldn't last long. "I can't tell if she's getting older and doesn't need the after-breakfast nap she's always relied on, or if she's internalizing what's going on around her and it's messing up her schedule."

"At this age, I'm leaning toward the first suggestion," Dean said. "Mostly because she sounds sincerely happy, and also because she still thinks people disappear when playing peekaboo."

Nicole hoped he was right. The idea her precious niece was upset without the words to express it, and therefore actively forming deep emotional scars from this experience, was too much to handle.

Outside her window, the sea dropped away as they climbed the sun-drenched hill toward the neighborhood where Cari last worked. The spectacular, unhindered view of the water was breathtaking. Deep blue ripples and white-crested waves stretched to the distant horizon, flickering and twinkling with sunlight.

She checked her side-view mirror on repeat and examined every passing car for signs of the black sedan, praying it wouldn't make another appearance. Surely the driver had somewhere else to be once in a while. He couldn't spend all his time patrolling the wealthiest area of town. Could he?

The street soon leveled out, and ancient trees swallowed her ocean view. A curvy, shaded stretch of road took its place. She blinked to adjust her eyes. Pretty beams of golden light dappled the darkened asphalt before her, filtered between the leaves and branches of reaching oaks.

Houses rose from extensively landscaped lots. Sprinklers nurturing the emerald lawns.

And all around them silence reigned.

Dean slowed as their destination came into view.

The woman who'd answered the door for Nicole stood in her driveway, unloading shopping bags from the trunk of a small blue convertible coupe.

Dean pulled into the space behind her and parked. "She doesn't know me," he said softly. "Give me a minute?"

Nicole nodded, hoping the woman wouldn't recognize her in the passenger seat. She lowered the visor and adjusted her oversize sunglasses. The blonde hadn't wanted to talk to Nicole. Maybe Dean could sway her. According to Finn, the police had already been to the house, and Nicole suspected this woman knew more than she was saying. If Dean was right about unseasoned criminals being likely to crack, this could be the conversation that changed everything.

The blonde watched Dean approach with obvious appreciation, a friendly smile on her pretty face.

Dean shook her hand.

Nicole leaned closer to the open window, straining to hear their voices over the wind and subtle sounds of her SUV's engine.

"Of course," the woman said, answering something Nicole had missed.

Dean removed his phone from his pocket and tapped the screen before turning the device to face her. He studied her as she turned her eyes to the offering, presumably a photo of Cari.

"Anything you can recall would be a big help," he said. "It's been a few days, and as you might know, these things tend to become dire as time passes. You can make a difference, maybe save a life."

Nicole's throat tightened.

"You could change the future for her family and her baby daughter."

The woman looked away, attention back on her packages, avoiding eye contact with Dean.

His clenching jaw suggested he'd noticed the change, too.

"I'm sorry," the woman said, closing the trunk and moving along her sidewalk to the home's front door. "I'm afraid I don't interact with party staff. I don't have the first clue what any of them look like, and I'm only dropping these things off. I have another appointment to get to. So if you'll excuse me."

Dean returned to the driver's seat and watched silently with Nicole as the woman struggled to unlock her door, dropping the keys twice before hurrying inside.

Nicole's thundering heart beat a rhythm she felt in her temples and beneath a palm pressed to her chest. "She knows something," she whispered.

"I'm inclined to agree," he said. "She definitely didn't want to talk about Cari or that party." He shifted into Reverse and stretched an arm across the back of her seat. "You okay?"

Nicole batted tear-blurred eyes, fighting the urge to jump out and pound on the woman's big fancy door. "When I talked to her, she said they didn't have a party."

The woman was lying.

Chapter Ten

Blakely gave a deep, groaning complaint, as Dean retreated from the driveway, still processing Nicole's words.

The homeowner told Nicole they hadn't had a party on the morning after Cari's disappearance. Two days later, she told Dean she didn't pay any attention to the staff, not that there wasn't a party.

What had she told Finn and his team?

Dean turned at the end of the block, driving deeper into the neighborhood, not ready to head home. "I'm going to pull over and shoot Finn a text. I'd like to hear how it went when he spoke with the homeowners. He should know she gave us two different stories. Everything about her body language indicated she was nervous. He'll say being approached by a stranger at home will do that, but I don't think her behavior should be written off. She didn't get twitchy until I mentioned the party."

Blakely screamed, and Nicole flinched.

"She's got to be tired, possibly hungry," Nicole said. "Maybe too warm and tired of being strapped into the car seat." She cranked the air-conditioning and rolled up the passenger window.

Dean followed her example, powering up his window as well, but Blakely's screaming continued.

The screen on Blakely's window stopped direct sunlight from getting to her, but it was still North Carolina in July.

He pulled into a small parking lot along the back side of the park where Nicole found Cari's jacket. "Do you want to get her out for a few minutes?"

"If you aren't in a hurry."

"None." In fact, everything inside him wanted to go back up the hill to the house he'd just left and demand answers until the woman caved. She had the feel of a weak link, and he knew how and where to apply pressure.

But that wasn't something he could do with Nicole and Blakely in tow.

"I'll feed and change her while you talk to Finn," Nicole said, already climbing out of the SUV.

Dean swiped his phone screen to life and dialed his brother. No reason to rush the chat with texts.

Finn answered quickly and confirmed he'd gotten the runaround from the homeowners as well. Their official statement being that they didn't have a party on the night of Cari's disappearance, but on the occasions when they had hosted events, they didn't interact with the staff. A tidy way to cover their change of story. Finn was chasing a lead to clarify, however, and that was good enough for Dean.

He disconnected the call feeling slightly better and immediately noticed the silence.

Nicole was visible in the SUV's side-view mirror, the baby no longer crying.

"It's quiet back there," he said, climbing out to join her. "How's it going?"

Nicole rocked from foot to foot, her niece sound asleep in the creamy cotton fabric of her sling. "She was dry and refused a bottle, but about two seconds in the sling and voilà. Now I can't get back into the car. She'll definitely wake up if I try to transfer her to the car seat too soon."

Dean smiled. "How about a walk in the park?"

Nicole looked at the expanse of lush, shaded grass. "Definitely."

He set his hand against the small of her back as they moved onto the cobblestoned path. The gentle pressure warmed her. A silly, nostalgic voice inside her wondered if this is what it would've been like for her and Dean if they'd stayed together. Would the baby in the sling be theirs? Would she have liked that? Would he?

Had he meant what he'd said to Blakely this morning? Words she hadn't been supposed to overhear. A confession of her continued importance to Dean, despite the time they'd spent apart.

She shook away the what-ifs that never led her anywhere good. "What did Finn say?" she asked instead, thankful for a reasonable distraction to her feelings.

Dean's small grin told her there was good news on the way, and her heart skipped.

"Finn says the couple denied having a party that night, and that they don't interact with the caterers when they do have a party. However, an officer working the desk recalls receiving a noise complaint from someone in the area around eleven thirty. The caller was a babysitter claiming there was a disturbance that woke the baby. She didn't have any specifics, possibly raised voices. Whatever it was ended before the call, and the kid's family returned before the neighborhood patrol car made it back around. The officer didn't see anything unusual. Finn's reaching out to the family who hired the sitter and to the patrolman on duty that night to see if one of them can shed more light. He's hoping the family will put him in touch with the babysitter as well."

Nicole smiled back. "He found a thread to pull."

Dean lifted a brow and a one hand, pointing a finger up the nearby hill. "I believe that's the back side of the home we just visited."

She followed his gaze to a distant two-story with a wrought iron fence and multilevel deck. "Yeah."

"And you found Cari's coat under a bench here."

She had. "You think Cari might've been part of the disturbance, running away from the party?"

"Maybe." Dean paused his strides and looked her over, gaze catching on her softly snoring niece. "How are you doing with her?" he asked. "I can carry her if she gets heavy. You're supposed to be taking it easy."

"I'm good. I'll let you know if I'm not."

They moved slowly through the shade, toward the home in question, each silently surveying the landscape.

Nicole tried to imagine her sister fleeing the party at night, running down the hill toward the trees, shucking her jacket to blend with the shadows.

Soon the oaks and pines formed an intentional row, and a small wooden sign in the shape of an arrow came into view. The words *Botanical Garden* were carved at its center.

Dean snapped a photo of the sign.

Nicole stared into the deepening shadows. "I didn't know the park included more than the trees, grass and benches."

"Let's see if Finn did." Dean tapped his screen, presumably sending a message with the photo before tucking the phone into his pocket. He set his hand against her back once more, and they followed the arrow onto a narrow brick-lined path.

Stone figures and bursts of greenery rose from the ground in neat patches. The trees grew sparse, and flowers bloomed in rows and planters. The babbling sound of water seemed to pull them in its direction.

A woman pushed an empty stroller at a snail's pace ten yards ahead of them. A toddler in a fairy costume trailed behind, waving a wand in one hand and carrying a juice box in the other.

If Cari were there, she would've speculated that they were looking into her future. Blakely would be that big before she was ready, and Cari would say she wished time would slow down.

Nicole's gaze fell to her niece once more.

Cari had to come home and see her baby grow up. No other future made any sense.

The fairy girl tugged the woman's shirt. "I want to see the bridge again."

The woman swept her onto her hip for a kiss. "Our picnic is over, and now it's time to go home."

Nicole's feet grew heavy, and something akin to hope twisted in her chest. She reached for Dean's hand, and he slowed. "The bridge."

"You want to see it, too?" he asked, a warm, if somewhat confused, expression on his face.

Nicole dropped his hand and dug her phone from her pocket. "Cari sent a photo of a bridge that night. I didn't think anything of it. I assumed it was part of the landscaping wherever she was, but if she ran here from the house—"

His eyes widened slightly, and he stepped closer, watching as she scrolled to the picture, then passed him the phone.

The bridge appeared only long enough for a few adults to stand shoulder to shoulder, and it stretched over a tiny stream filled with stones. Exactly the kind of thing Nicole could imagine finding in the Botanical Garden.

Dean turned in a small circle, scanning the area. His gaze lifted to the woman and child, now significantly farther away. "Come on." He clutched Nicole's hand and headed for the pair on long quick legs.

Nicole cradled Blakely's sleeping body to her torso, struggling to ease the impact of her steps.

Dean released her hand when the woman and child took notice of their rushed approach. "Excuse me."

The woman set the child down and smiled. "Hello."

"Can you tell me if this bridge is somewhere around here?" he asked, extending the phone in her direction and cutting straight to the point. "If not here, maybe somewhere in the neighborhood?"

She frowned at his urgency, but gave the phone a look. "Oh, sure. That's the fairy bridge." Her gaze swept cautiously to Nicole, and she lifted a finger in the direction of another path. "It's at the end of the brook."

"Thank you," Nicole said, reaching for Dean once more. "Take Blakely?"

Her side burned and ached after their short speed walk. She couldn't keep up the pace with her niece in tow. Maybe not even without her.

Dean obliged without question, intervening immediately when the act of raising her arms caused Nicole to wince. She needed water and another round of painkillers, but that would have to wait until they'd visited the fairy bridge.

They excused themselves with small waves and quickly changed directions, following the sounds of water to a small pool. A narrow trickling stream spilled into a circular goldfish pond at one end. The water traveled around moss-covered rocks and over a sandy floor that began a short distance away.

"I can't believe all this is back here," Dean said, heading for the other end of the stream.

Nicole pressed a palm to her aching side. "I know.

I thought the park ended at the tree line. I assumed everything beyond that belonged to nearby homes."

He adjusted Blakely in his arms when she fussed softly, then sent a hopeful look in Nicole's direction. "If I left the house on the hill and needed somewhere to hide, I'd have come here."

Her heart rate sped. She'd thought something similar on their way into the Botanical Garden, but if Cari had come here, where was she now? Nicole couldn't let herself think about what it would mean if her sister was still nearby but hadn't come home.

"Hey," Dean said, drawing her eyes to meet his. "She's not here. The lady and the kid would've seen her. This is another clue, and that's a good thing. It could bring us one step closer to finding her."

The dim glow of twinkle lights wrapped around the wooden handrail was suddenly a beacon.

"This is it," she said. "It's the same as in the photo."

Dean raised his phone and snapped a pic. "I'm sending this to Finn, along with the coordinates. He should probably get down here and poke around."

Dean held Blakely protectively in one arm as he slipped into PI mode and explored the space around the wooden structure. He photographed the collection of footprints fanning out in every direction, crisscrossing over one another on the soft ground.

His phone rang as he crouched at the water's edge, peering into the stream.

Nicole's head grew light as she scanned the larger picture, noticing the strings of unlit twinkle lights wrapped around tree trunks and limbs for the first time. It was probably beautiful here at night, when all the lights were on.

Her sister had been right here, on this spot, before she'd vanished.

Nicole's breaths grew shallow, and she bumbled to the bridge and sat. The planks were solid and sturdy beneath her, unlike her trembling body and legs.

Dean rose. "What's wrong? Are you hurting?"

Nicole concentrated on pulling oxygen into her lungs. "I needed to rest," she muttered. "That's all."

Dean snapped out of work mode, worried eyes back on her. "I can take you home. Unless you need a doctor. Are you hurting?" His attention fell to her hand, pressed against her side.

"I just need a minute. I'm okay."

"Finn's on the way," Dean said, outstretching a hand to help her back up. "He can do this. I'll take you home."

"No." The word flew from her lips like a slap.

Dean's head reared back, and Blakely's limbs flailed. He lowered his hand. "Okay," he said softly. "We'll wait."

Nicole scooted across the boards, pulling her knees closer to her chest and resting her back against a beam that supported the handrail. Something dark caught her eye between the slats at her feet. She rocked forward, then onto her hands and knees, lowering her face to the wood for a better look. Beneath her, a mound of smooth gray rocks ran along the water's edge.

Something dark and familiar rested atop the stones.

"Nicole?" Dean's voice was high and urgent. "Are you okay?"

"There's a cell phone."

Dean followed her gaze, brows lifting when he saw it, too. "Can you hold Blakely?"

She nodded, rearranging herself to cuddle her niece.

He passed the baby into her arms, then moved onto the rocks beside the bridge. Water lapped at the soles of his shoes as he squatted and stretched an arm beneath her.

She watched between the slats as his fingers closed around the device.

A moment later he returned to her with Cari's phone in hand.

Chapter Eleven

Thirty minutes later, Dean rocked Blakely in his arms outside the SUV, mind spinning with possible scenarios to explain how Cari's phone had landed beneath the bridge. Had she dropped it while on the run?

Nicole reclined in the passenger seat, sipping from a bottle of water Finn had provided and waiting for Cari's phone to charge.

Finn leaned against the vehicle's hood, arms crossed, scrutinizing the scene at large. "No signs of the black sedan or Mikey."

Neighbors and lookie-loos had gathered in clusters on the grass, taking videos and chattering about what the police were doing in their neighborhood and at the Botanical Center.

Dean had listened for a while. The speculation ran from a murder suspect hiding among the oaks to a hunt for stolen property.

Nicole pressed the water bottle to her temple. "Is that a good thing or a bad thing?"

"Bad," Finn said. "If one of them showed up, at least I'd have the chance to question him. Or maybe the fact they aren't here means they haven't heard about this yet, which is good."

Dean agreed. He crouched slightly, peering at Nicole through the open window. "How's the phone doing?"

She pressed the button to illuminate the lock screen. "Almost five percent."

"That's enough," he said. "Let's try it."

It'd taken forever for someone to show up with a charger that worked with Cari's phone. Waiting for it to gain enough strength to turn on seemed to take even longer.

Nicole tapped the screen with shaky fingers. "It doesn't think I'm her," she said, moving the device in front of her face. They'd hoped facial recognition would assume the sisters were one and the same. Their physical similarities were remarkable to the human eye, but apparently not close enough to fool the phone. "And it doesn't know my fingerprint."

They'd expected that but agreed in advance it was worth a try.

"I have no idea what her password could be." Nicole sighed.

Finn grinned. "It's okay. Leave it to charge. Take the time to think a little longer. If you can't unlock it before you head home, the tech lab will give it a try. They're pretty good over there."

Dean felt the weight of disappointment on his shoulders. He'd hoped the facial recognition would work. He'd seen his brothers unlock one another's devices that way in the past.

"Why don't y'all head home?" Finn suggested. "I'm sure Blakely would like that. It's hot as Hades out here, and you're probably all hungry by now. It's been a day."

Nicole turned wary eyes on Dean, as if asking him to decide.

"Whatever you want to do," he said.

If she wasn't ready to leave the scene, he could probably find someone to make a trip to the nearest store for more water, food and pain pills. He could run the air conditioner in the SUV to give Nicole and Blakely a respite from the heat. And he could play with the baby when she woke, so Nicole could take the time she needed to process their day.

Whatever they decided, he could make it work.

Finn reached through her open window and nudged her shoulder. "I promise to call if I learn anything useful. Or if I get the phone unlocked. Matter of fact, once the phone's unlocked, I'll bring it to your place, and we can go through any contacts and messages of interest. Do you know if she kept her location tracking enabled?"

Nicole shook her head. "I'm not sure. Maybe."

Dean gave his brother a nod of appreciation, then buckled Blakely into her seat. "Why don't you stop by Nicole's apartment when you leave here?" he suggested. "You can fill us in then, and Nicole can give the phone's pass code another try."

Finn patted the roof. "Will do." His gaze dropped to Nicole's tired face. "Take care. Rest. Hydrate."

She lifted her bottle of water and gave it a wiggle.

He smiled. "I guess I'll see y'all in a bit then."

The drive back to Nicole's apartment was long and silent. Dean watched every passing car for signs of the black sedan. The air was heavier. Suffocating despite the blasting air-conditioning.

And if he felt this way, he could only imagine what Nicole was feeling.

Once someone was missing three days, the odds of finding them significantly lowered. Any evidence discovered from this point forward would be polluted at best, unidentifiable and useless at worst. Time was everything, and the window for a successful recovery was closing fast.

He pulled into Nicole's designated parking spot outside her building and unloaded Blakely from the car. Her big brown eyes were open, and her face twisted into a smile. "Someone's up," he said, curling her against his chest. "Have a good rest, Little Miss?"

Nicole climbed out, one hand pressed to her side.

They crossed the lot to the building, where a moving truck had backed up to the door. A kid with floppy hair and a sweaty T-shirt kicked a stopper loose but held the door for Dean and Nicole when he noticed their approach.

"Hey, man," he said, making room for them to pass.

Dean looked him over, unease creeping along his spine. "You just move in?"

"Nah. My aunt. She's in 310 now. The family's helping her get settled. You live in the building?"

"I do," Nicole said. "Tell your aunt I said welcome."

The kid lifted the stopper from the ground and tossed it in the air, catching it before moving toward the stairs. "Will do. Nice meeting y'all."

"Hey," Dean called, hating the instinctual churning in his gut. "Was this door propped open for long?"

"Not too long. A couple hours maybe," the kid said. "Made it easier to get things inside from the truck when our hands were full."

Dean grunted.

The kid bunched his features. "Sorry, man. Was that some kind of policy violation?"

"No." Nicole reached for Dean, giving his arm a tight squeeze, clearly sensing whatever it was that had him on high alert.

"Thanks," Dean told the kid, relieving him from the conversation.

He took Nicole's hand and moved slowly toward her apartment door, adjusting Blakely in his arms. "I don't like knowing that door was propped open."

"I'm sure someone from that kid's family was coming and going the whole time."

"Maybe," he said. "But none of them would know if anyone walking inside actually belonged here."

She didn't argue, and he took the lead moving toward her apartment.

Several steps later, they stopped short when her door came into view.

The thin wooden trim around the frame was cracked, and the door was slightly ajar.

Nicole gasped, and his protective instincts went

up like a cloak, covering him wholly and sending his body into autopilot.

He passed Blakely into Nicole's arms. "Stay close," he said, unwilling to leave her unprotected in the hallway, even for a minute. "Text Finn." He nudged the door open before stepping inside and removing his sidearm.

Nicole pulled the sling from her bag and slid her niece inside, then unearthed her cell phone.

The living room and kitchen were visible and empty, lit by the midday light through an abundance of windows. Each room appeared untouched.

Dean raised a flattened palm to instruct Nicole to stay put. He'd given the same silent request dozens of times when they'd dated, though typically during family baseball games.

She nodded in understanding and pressed her back against the door frame while he moved on.

He inched carefully down the hall, quickly clearing the bathroom, then Nicole's room, and finally arriving in Cari's space.

A creaking floorboard spun him on a dime, weapon raised to half-mast before confirming it was Nicole. "All clear," he said, returning the gun to its holster.

Her eyes were wide and her mouth open as she took in the scene before her. A whispered cuss broke on her lips.

"Yeah."

Cari's room had been destroyed. All Dean's work, all the tidy piles and organized rows of her personal content, were scattered. The mattress was undressed and askew. The closet's contents purged. Her laptop gone.

They'd been at the Botanical Center in another neighborhood searching for clues while Cari's abductor, or his minion, had been breaking into their home.

NICOLE SWORE AGAIN, a luxury habit most second-grade teachers couldn't afford. But—

The word escaped again.

She backed into the hallway, realizing Cari's room was a crime scene. Maybe the entire apartment was a crime scene.

Nicole's life was becoming a crime scene.

She kept moving until the kitchen came into view, then she strapped Blakely into her high chair and poured a glass of water.

Dean stayed on her heels.

She drained the glass, then poured another.

Dean crossed into the living room, relaying the details of the break-in to someone by phone. "They were looking for something," he said, pulling the black duffel Austin had brought him from its place in the coat closet. He pinched the phone between his shoulder and cheek, then retrieved a pair of blue latex gloves. "I don't know. They have the laptop. I shouldn't have left it here after what happened outside the pizza shop." He grimaced and returned the bag to the closet. "I keep underestimating the level of danger we're facing. These are motivated criminals, which tells me the stakes are big." His gaze jumped to Nicole, and he froze. "I'm going to call you back."

"One Minute" Survey

You get up to **FOUR** books <u>and</u> a Mystery Gift...

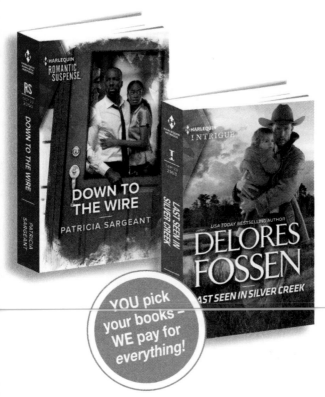

Dear Reader,

Your opinions are important to us. So if you'll participate in our fast and free "One Minute" Survey, YOU can pick up to four wonderful books that WE pay for when you try the Harlequin Reader Service!

As a leading publisher of women's fiction, we'd love to hear from you. That's why we promise to reward you for completing our survey.

IMPORTANT: Please complete the survey and return it. We'll send your Free Books and a Free Mystery Gift right away. And we pay for shipping and handling too! *We pay for EVERYTHING!*

Try **Harlequin® Romantic Suspense** and get 2 books featuring heart-racing page-turners with unexpected plot twists and irresistible chemistry that will keep you guessing to the very end.

Try **Harlequin Intrigue® Larger-Print** and get 2 books featuring action-packed stories that will keep you on the edge of your seat. Solve the crime and deliver justice at all costs.

Or TRY BOTH!

Thank you again for participating in our "One Minute" Survey. It really takes just a minute (or less) to complete the survey... and your free books and gift will be well worth it!

If you continue with your subscription, you can look forward to curated monthly shipments of brand-new books from your selected series, always at a discount off the cover price! Plus you can cancel any time. So don't miss out, return your One Minute Survey today to get your Free books.

Pam Powers

"One Minute" Survey

GET YOUR FREE BOOKS AND A FREE GIFT!

✓ Complete this Survey   ✓ Return this survey

1 Do you try to find time to read every day?

☐ YES   ☐ NO

2 Do you prefer stories with suspenseful storylines?

☐ YES   ☐ NO

3 Do you enjoy having books delivered to your home?

☐ YES   ☐ NO

4 Do you share your favorite books with friends?

☐ YES   ☐ NO

YES! I have completed the above "One Minute" Survey. Please send me my Free Books and a Free Mystery Gift (worth over \$20 retail). I understand that I am under no obligation to buy anything, as explained on the back of this card.

☐ **Harlequin® Romantic Suspense**
240/340 CTI G2AD

☐ **Harlequin Intrigue® Larger-Print**
199/399 CTI G2AD

☐ **BOTH**
240/340 & 199/399
CTI G2AE

FIRST NAME

LAST NAME

ADDRESS

APT.#

CITY

STATE/PROV.

ZIP/POSTAL CODE

EMAIL ☐ Please check this box if you would like to receive newsletters and promotional emails from Harlequin Enterprises ULC and its affiliates. You can unsubscribe anytime.

HI/HRS-1123-OM

He pushed his phone into his pocket and headed her way, his gaze never leaving hers.

She wasn't sure what he saw, but she felt like an alternate version of herself. Something hollow and surreal. Because this wasn't her life. She was a second-grade teacher in a quaint coastal town. Her sister was happy and healthy, a new mom who made good choices.

Nicole's eyes closed, and strong arms curved around her, bringing her cheek to rest on a broad, familiar chest. "This isn't real," she whispered, wishing she could make the words true.

Dean widened his stance, wrapping her up in him, shielding and cocooning her, then resting his cheek on top of her head. "Finn's on the way. So is Austin. We're going to dust the door and broken jamb for prints and sort Cari's room again. We'll need you to see if anything's missing. I just went through everything a couple of nights ago, so I'll be familiar. Together, we should know if anything other than the laptop was taken."

Her numb mind revived with his declaration. And another mental blow came fast and hard. "Cari was logged in to all her social media. Whoever took the laptop will have access to everything just like we did."

"They'll have to get past the lock screen," Dean said. "If we can unlock her cell phone, we can probably log her out of everything connected to her main account. The computer's lock screen should buy us some time. You're the only one who knew that password."

"Me and Cari," she said, hating all the ways someone holding her sister hostage could force the password from her. And to compound her pain, the laptop
suddenly felt like her last connection to Cari. As if
access to her sister's online world had been a tether.

Now that string had been cut, too.

Heavy footfalls and familiar voices echoed outside
the apartment door a moment before Dean's brothers
knocked. Dean released her, and an icy chill rushed
over her in his absence.

Then the processing of the newest crime scene
began.

Nicole and Blakely watched as the Beaumonts
dusted for fingerprints, took endless photos, docu-
mented every step and eventually went to interview
neighbors. Austin volunteered to knock on other first-
floor doors. Finn went to find the young man Nicole
and Dean had met on their way in and speak with his
family on the third floor.

Dean closed the door behind his brothers, then
crouched before Nicole on the recliner.

She mindlessly bounced a small stuffed bunny that
had once belonged to Cari on her niece's chubby legs.
Blakely giggled and kicked her feet in delight.

"Your landlord's been notified about the break-
in. My brothers are going to replace your locks and
repair the splintered jamb," Dean said. "They'll re-
organize Cari's room before they go. We can take a
look at that when you're ready."

"Sounds good." She wanted to hop to her feet and

get started now, but the out-of-body sensation hadn't fully gone away, and her side was burning.

He raised a hand bearing two more over-the-counter pain pills. "You never had a chance to take these."

She took them immediately with a swig of water from her nearby glass.

"There's something else," Dean said, carefully. His tone put her further on edge.

She raised her brows, unable to voice the question. *What else has gone wrong now?*

"Given the events of the day, I think it would be wise for you and Blakely to leave the apartment for a few days. Maybe until Cari returns, but at least until the danger stops coming every time we stand still long enough to take a deep breath."

Nicole nodded. "Mom's coming in from Charleston today," she said. "She'll want to see Blakely, and I want to see her." She couldn't afford a hotel room for more than a night or two. She squinted at the man before her, turning his words over in her mind. "Are you asking me to move to the ranch?"

"No." He cleared his throat. "I thought you could stay with me."

Nicole's mouth opened, then shut without comment.

"My cabin has enough space," he said, apparently under the impression she needed to be sold on the offer, as if she hadn't been about to scream out her sincere thanks. "My address isn't listed anywhere," he pressed on. "Austin and I went to significant lengths to protect our privacy when purchasing our homes.

You'll be comfortable. You're familiar with the space. I'm sure Mama will absolutely inundate us with food once she knows you're there, and best of all you'll be able to rest. When you feel like getting some fresh air, you can wander my property. Blakely can play on a picnic blanket under the trees. And I can protect you both."

Nicole didn't love the idea of leaving the home she shared with Cari, but she wanted Blakely to be safe. She wanted to stop worrying over every floorboard creak and little sound outside her window. And she didn't hate the memory of Dean's home only having one bed. Not that anything would happen if they shared it, but she knew she'd sleep better with him beside her, and having his arms around her earlier had only made her long for him to embrace her again. "Did you ever set up the guest room?"

Something like heat flashed in his eyes, there and gone before she could be certain what she'd seen. "No, but I thought we could put a portable crib in there for Blakely. You'd be right next door. I'd sleep on the couch. I'm not suggesting anything—" his cheeks darkened slightly, the blush plainly visible thanks to his morning shave "—that would make you uncomfortable."

"I know," she said. "I know you."

Their gazes locked, and the temperature rose. Her heart rate climbed for new reasons as she fell deeper into the depths of his baby blues.

Of course Dean Beaumont would willingly sleep

on his own couch instead of sharing his king-size bed if she asked. That was just the kind of man he was.

But Nicole had no intention of asking.

Chapter Twelve

Nicole relaxed as they neared Dean's cabin, feeling lighter and more hopeful than she had in a few days. Dean's home would be safer for her and Blakely. And if Blakely was safe, Nicole could breathe easier, unwind and maybe think of something useful to help the Beaumonts find her sister.

She admired the familiar gravel lane of his driveway, long and narrow, lined in tall leafy trees and luxurious shade.

A large white pickup sat at the far end, parked behind Dean's big truck.

"Well, that shouldn't surprise me at all," he said, sliding her SUV into the space beside his vehicle. "My parents beat us here."

Nicole smiled as his mama started down the porch steps in their direction, arms and smile open wide. His dad followed more slowly, letting his wife take her usual enthusiastic lead.

"You ready for this?" Dean asked. A twinkle she hadn't seen in a long while danced in his soulful blue eyes.

She'd missed that twinkle.

"Absolutely." Nicole climbed out and rounded the hood, a dozen emotions pressing her forward. She'd missed his parents immensely. They were the family everyone wanted but few had. Her folks loved her, she knew, but the things they'd gone through with Cari had changed them from the people they were when Nicole was small. Her mom was distant now, thanks to the emotional walls she'd erected for her survival in the worst of times. The same walls that had pushed their dad away. And though Cari had been clean for years, their mom's barriers remained firmly in place, as had their father's absence. Part of her wondered what he would do when their mother told him about Cari as she'd promised to do. Probably nothing. It was hard knowing their family hadn't always been that way.

Mrs. Beaumont, on the other hand, seemed softer and more tenderhearted with every soul she nurtured. "Look at you," she called, engulfing Nicole in a strong, motherly hug. She smelled of lilacs and cookies. Her long salt-and-pepper hair was wild and frizzed with humidity. Her soft cheeks felt like home against Nicole's skin. "Oh. How I've missed you."

"I've missed you, too."

She stepped back, taking Nicole's hands in hers and looking her over head to toe. "Beautiful as ever. And from what I hear, every bit as strong."

Nicole swallowed a lump of grief and pride. "I'm trying. Dean's doing the real work."

His mother's warm brown eyes slid to her son.

"Well, you two always did make one heck of a team." Whatever else she'd intended to say was lost as Dean pulled Blakely from her car seat.

"Oh!" Mrs. Beaumont released Nicole, heat-seeking maternal radar locked on the baby. "Sweet precious darling," she cooed, already heading her way. "Dean Beaumont, you were born for this look," she said, rising on her toes to kiss Dean's cheek as he cradled Blakely. "A-plus daddy material, right here." She patted his chest, stole a look in Nicole's direction and winked. Then she smoothly relieved Dean of his charge. "I'll take it from here. You can see to Nicole."

Nicole laughed, and Dean went to stand at her side.

Together, they watched his parents coo and fuss over Blakely, clearly in their happiest of zones.

"You want to go inside?" he asked, resting a palm against the curve of her spine.

The gentle touch warmed her heart, the scene around them reminding her of another life.

She nodded when words failed, and he led her to the door.

His folks fell in line behind them. Mrs. Beaumont carried Blakely while Mr. Beaumont hauled a slew of thermal casserole totes and grocery bags from the porch.

Thirty minutes later, the kitchen table and counters were covered in homemade foods and covered dishes. His parents had brought enough to feed an army and insisted on leaving it all for leftovers, and his brothers, who she assumed would be over soon.

Nicole sipped a tall glass of sweet tea and nibbled at an array of fruits, cheeses and sliced veggies.

Dean sat opposite her, watching with an intensity that suggested his mind wasn't on anything but her. When his gaze flickered to her mouth and neck, she was sure she could feel the press of lips there as well.

Mrs. Beaumont bustled through the kitchen, clapping Dean on his shoulder as she passed. She rinsed a teething ring in the sink after Blakely tossed it on the floor. "I'm glad you two let us know about the community forming under the highways. Lincoln and Josie delivered three dozen sandwiches that night, plus chips, pretzels, water and all the fruits I had on hand. They said those folks took everything they offered and were glad for it."

Dean dragged his attention to his mother as she hurried back to Blakely. "Nicole and I drove by there this morning and everyone was gone. Did Lincoln or Josie mention if it looked as if they were packing up?"

She frowned. "No. Josie thought we might see one or two of them at the ranch soon. She did the talking, I'd imagine."

Dean rubbed the back of his neck. "I forgot to mention their absence to Finn. It might not mean anything, or maybe it does."

"He's on his way here," she said. "I sent him and Austin messages about the food. You know they can't resist my cowboy casserole or cobbler."

Nicole sampled a fresh strawberry and smiled. The inside of Dean's cabin was more than just a respite. It was another universe, where it was safe to let her guard down, because everything was going to be just fine. And she'd needed this more than she knew.

Mr. Beaumont made silly faces at Blakely while his wife was away. He tapped her nose with one finger, making her squeal in delight, then he snapped pictures of her with his phone.

Mrs. Beaumont returned to the mix, freshly cleaned teether in hand. "You know," she said, "when things aren't going the way we'd hoped, it's important to focus on the good. This little one right here is all good."

Mr. Beaumont snapped another photo. "She looks just like Cari. Just like you and your mama, too. Look at these curls."

Blakely kicked and flailed, exercising her chunky limbs and adoring the attention.

"Will you or Blakely need anything?" Mrs. Beaumont asked Nicole. "We heard about the break-in and know you plan to stay a while. I can't imagine you fit everything you both need into that little SUV. We're happy to come back with supplies, baby gear, wine, dinner and a movie."

His dad chuckled. "Mary, let them be."

She frowned.

The older couple exchanged a long look and beat of silence, then his dad's attention returned to Dean. "Do you need help setting up the guest room? We've got twin beds in storage at the ranch."

"No." His mother cut him off with another look and an elbow. "I'm sure they can work that out."

Nicole did her best not to laugh. Dean looked absolutely horrified. A teen embarrassed by his parents.

"Nicole is taking my room," he said flatly. "We'll set up the portable crib for Blakely in the guest room. I'll take the couch. That'll keep me near the front door in case anyone drops by late, as my brothers tend to do, and I'll be able to take calls and work without disrupting their rest."

His dad nodded in approval.

His mom rolled her eyes.

Nicole decided to give him a break and change the subject. "My mom's on her way. Have you spoken with her?"

"Yep," Mrs. Beaumont said. "And speaking of guests, we should probably get back."

Mr. Beaumont carried Blakely to Dean, having been warned over dinner that Nicole was supposed to take it easy. "I'd love to stay and play with this little nugget all evening, but we've got a nearly full ranch this week, and I can't be gone too long. Who knows what Lincoln would do if one of the ranch's residents mouthed off to him or Josie."

His mother groaned. "That hypothetical kid would be better off provoking Lincoln than Josie. Otherwise he'll get two retaliations."

"If we come home to find anyone mucking stalls or doing push-ups, we'll know what happened," his dad said.

Nicole's smile widened. Lincoln never had much to say to her, but she'd always liked him. She liked Josie, too, though she was young, and they'd had extremely little in common the last time they'd met. Still, she hoped to see them both again soon.

She walked the Beaumonts to the door and hugged them each goodbye, already missing her former surrogate parents and eager to squeeze her mother the moment she got in.

DEAN PUT THE last of his mama's food into the refrigerator just before seven that evening. His brothers Finn and Austin sat with Nicole at the living room table. As promised, they'd arrived for dinner. The group had talked for hours, discussing life and Cari's disappearance in an intertwined ebb and flow. They'd gotten reacquainted while admiring Blakely and trying passwords on Cari's cell phone. The device continued to lock after each fail. The penalty time grew longer as well.

Finn drummed his thumbs against the table's edge. "If the phone's still locked when I head back to the station, I'll take it to the tech lab. Either way, we'll figure it out."

Dean appreciated Finn's words of encouragement. Nicole had been beating herself up for not knowing the password. She'd tried everything she could think of, and she was wearing down.

Finn was good at looking on the bright side. At twenty-five and relentlessly positive, he usually frustrated everyone with his silver linings. But Dean was thankful for Finn tonight. He'd kept Nicole engaged and busy, making notes of all the passwords she'd tried and lists of possibilities for when the device let them try again. Birth dates. Special occasion dates. Patterns on the keypad.

"What else is new?" Austin asked, looking bored and mildly restless as usual.

"It didn't take long to get the details on Mikey Likey," Finn said. "His real name is Michael Litchfield. He's twenty-seven and a known dope dealer with a long list of priors, though nothing big that stuck. I'm guessing he took one look at Dean and assumed he was an undercover cop. He said he thought someone might be after him, but I doubt anyone would confuse this big brother for a thug."

Dean crossed his arms, unaffected. Finn had probably meant the comment as a joke or jab, but not looking like a criminal was just fine with him.

"I spoke with Mikey's boss at Ricky Rocket's," Finn continued. "He said Mikey's a good worker, typically reliable, but he hasn't been back since being chased."

Nicole shifted on her seat, lacing and unlacing her fingers on the tabletop. "He told us we put a target on his back by showing up. I hope nothing bad has happened to him."

"Uh." Finn wrinkled his nose and forehead. "I think Mikey has done a bang-up job of painting that target all by himself."

"What did his coworkers think of him?" Dean asked. Maybe the face Mikey showed his boss wasn't the same one he showed his peers. "Any chance they had another perspective?"

"Nope. Everyone I spoke with genuinely thinks he's a good guy, even the ones who knew about his questionable side hustles. Unfortunately, no one seemed to know who he spent time with or where he went outside work."

Dean considered that, then asked the question popping into mind. "Could someone at the pizzeria be the one arranging the catering?"

"I doubt it," Finn said. "No one on staff, even the owner, has the kind of money or connections needed to fit the model we're building. The home parties are elite and exclusive. A whole other world."

Austin stretched his long legs under the table, grunting and staring at his cell phone. He'd been texting with someone off and on for a while but hadn't looked up to fill anyone in on what he was doing.

Dean had decided ten minutes ago that whatever his brother was up to had better be good, otherwise his behavior was unacceptably rude.

All he'd shared with the group so far was a thorough background check on the couple from the alleged party location. Mr. and Mrs. Tippin. Austin had gone door to door talking to the neighbors and kept a map with the feedback. He'd also dug into the couple's lives online and created a file with mostly superfluous details.

"What'd you learn about the Tippins?" Nicole asked. Her wide brown eyes moved from Finn to Austin, eager for information from any source.

"As far as I can tell," Finn said, "the Tippins have been married eleven years. Mrs. Tippin doesn't work outside the home, and Mr. Tippin sells high-end cars."

"He's a manager at the luxury automobile dealership that overlooks the sound," Austin said.

Nicole chewed her bottom lip. "He was getting into a fancy sports car when I saw him."

"Dealer plate?"

"I didn't notice. I was still hoping Cari would pop up and apologize for being late and worrying me."

His brothers grunted and nodded.

Dean leaned against the kitchen countertop, unexpectedly winded by a sudden pang of mixed emotions. He hated the reason for tonight's gathering, but spending the evening with his family, Nicole and Blakely had been nice. It'd felt good and right. He wanted to spend hundreds more evenings like these, though under better circumstances. And he couldn't help wondering if Nicole might be interested in that, too.

Finn's brows rose, and Dean realized he'd been staring.

He shook his head to indicate he'd been lost in thought. Nothing more.

"Austin found the babysitter from the phone call," Finn said.

"What?" Dean's eyes snapped to Austin's.

Austin frowned. "I just said that. Didn't you hear me?"

"No." He extended a hand in his brother's direction. "Sorry. One more time."

Austin straightened, more amused than irritated and seeing more than Dean would've preferred. As usual. "I asked every family near the Botanical Center if they were home or away on the night Cari disappeared. Eventually I found two couples who'd gone out and left their kids with babysitters. I got the babysitters' contact information and left messages. I've been texting with one of those sitters for about twenty minutes. She's the one who called to report a noise violation, and she just told me she took a video with her cell phone that night. I'm waiting for it to load. You need to upgrade your internet package."

"I live in the woods. This is a good speed."

"Mine's better." Austin's gaze flickered back to his phone. "Here we go." He rose and moved to stand beside Nicole, sharing his screen with her and Finn.

Dean went to join them.

The image on-screen was dark and quiet, save for a soft voice-over. "Look at all these cars," a woman said. "There's even a freaking valet." The video panned through a closed window, over the expanse of grass at the park and twinkle lights from the Botanical Center, then to the small lot, wholly filled with cars.

"They valeted the cars," Finn said. "No wonder no one on the street recalled a party."

"Smart," Nicole said. "No one would be at the park after dark. The lot was empty and close. This took planning."

Dean set a hand on her shoulder, lending his strength. "Do you see Cari's car?"

She squinted. "It's dark, but I don't think so. And not from this distance."

The video ended and Finn huffed. "Well, I can't wait to take this to the Tippins. Maybe they'll change their tune about that party they didn't have. Send this to me," he said, addressing Austin.

"Done."

Finn tapped his phone. "All right. I'm pushing it over to the tech lab for enhancement. If they can pick up any license plate number, or even a partial, we can try to match it with a vehicle make and model, then go poking party guests until we get what we need. We might even be able to ID one of the valets. Then I can find out who hired them." Finn pushed onto his feet. "I'm going to head back to the station and try to get this moving."

Austin followed suit. "I'm going to visit my informants. See if anyone's heard anything about Mikey."

Dean walked his brother to the door. "Good luck proving the cars at the park were valeted from the Tippins' home."

Finn offered a bland expression. "I've got this."

"I guess I'll hold down the fort." Dean itched to grab his truck keys or call shotgun, but his work was at the cabin. He had to keep Nicole and Blakely safe and comfortable.

Finn's lips quirked. "Good luck playing fort."

Austin snorted, then clapped Dean on the back as he passed into the night.

Nicole moved to his side, brushing against him as she waved goodbye to his brothers.

His body ignited at her touch, and he stepped away.

Another night alone with Nicole. Knowing she was in his bed?

He was going to need all the luck he could get.

Chapter Thirteen

Nicole woke to soft shuffling sounds outside Dean's bedroom door. A door she'd left open in case he reconsidered his night on the couch. She wouldn't have minded feeling his arms around her again. Each time he'd embraced her this week, it'd felt a little more like coming home.

She'd wondered a thousand times how he was really doing. Had he fully healed from their breakup? She used to think she had, but spending time with Dean like this had her wondering if all she'd really done was fill her time with other things. Staying busy had always been her way to manage pain. Ignore it, and it might not go away, but at least she wasn't thinking about it.

The floorboards creaked, and Nicole sat up. The world outside was dark, and according to the clock on the nightstand, it was after three. Was Dean still awake?

Soft white light was visible though the open doorway, drawing her from the bed and into the cabin beyond. Goose bumps scattered over her bare arms and legs as she left the warm blanket nest in favor of seeing Dean.

The air stilled as she walked, and tension climbed over her. For the briefest moment she feared the person she heard moving around in the next room wasn't Dean.

He stepped into view from the kitchen, and her heart fluttered. His brows rose in surprise. "Everything okay? Did I wake you?"

"Yeah," she whispered, crossing her arms over the soft cotton T-shirt she'd chosen for a nightgown. There was something nonsensically stunning about the intimacy of meeting him in the night, both in pajamas and bare feet. And her thoughts stalled.

Her hungry gaze traveled over him, eating up the sight. Pale gray cotton sleep pants hung low on his hips. His shirt clung to the angles and plane of his chest, emphasizing his perfectly lean torso.

"Sorry," he said. "Was it the light?"

She blinked, mentally rewinding the previous exchange, attempting to make sense of his question. "Oh. No. You didn't wake me." She ran a hand through her messy hair. "I meant I'm okay. Nothing's wrong. I'm just a light sleeper now, thanks to having a baby in the house." And before Blakely's arrival, a very sick and immensely pregnant little sister.

The constant anxiety that came with knowing that same sister had recently vanished only made it harder to rest.

"Do you want some tea?" he offered. "I was just putting on some coffee. I can heat water for you."

She nodded. "Okay." Her side was sore and her body fatigued, but she wasn't ready to go back to bed.

Dean went to the kitchen and pulled a bottle of pain pills from the cabinet where he kept a first aid kit and tea bags. He passed the bottle to her before filling a kettle with water and setting it on the stove.

"Thanks." She accepted the pills. Staying ahead of the pain was key for faster healing. Or at least that had been what the hospital staff told Cari after delivering Blakely.

He placed a pod in his single-cup coffee brewer, and his earlier words circled back through her mind.

"You're drinking coffee. Have you gotten any sleep?"

He offered a cautious smile. "I don't sleep much."

Her stomach tightened, knowing the reason and unsure if it was okay to ask. "Because of Cari's case? Or has it been like this since before? Since the missing boy?"

"The latter."

"Do you want to talk about it?"

Dean's expression hardened before he looked away.

She didn't blame him. This was how too many similar conversations had begun, and those chats had never ended well. Collectively, they'd led to the end of their relationship.

She stepped forward and wrapped her arms around him, providing him the comfort he always gave to her. "You know, for whatever it's worth now, more than a year too late, I'm sorry for what you went through. I'm sorry you're still going through it, and I don't know how you keep going, but I'm really glad you do."

She'd realized at some point in the last few days

that investigators and law officers had to see and do things in the name of justice that most people never thought about and wouldn't survive if they did. People like Dean and his brothers dedicated their lives to protecting and serving others. But who protected them?

She hadn't when she'd had the opportunity. Dean had been hurting, and she'd chosen to walk away.

His frame stiffened for the duration of a heartbeat before he sank into the embrace.

Nicole breathed him in, absorbing his warmth and familiar scent. She could identify his soap, shampoo and fabric softener by smell alone, and for months after their breakup, someone would pass her on the street or in the store and she'd spin in search of Dean.

She reveled in the strength of his heartbeat beneath her ear, and the way his fingers splayed across her back. One big palm skated up and down her spine, soothing and caressing. He stroked long, loose curls away from her face and over her shoulder, skimming his hand against the tender skin at the base of her neck. She shivered.

"I've missed this," he whispered. "I've missed you. Every day."

The kettle's lid rattled a warning, and Dean released her, stepping away to remove the pot from the heat before it whistled. The words *I've missed you, too* stuck in her throat, but the moment had passed. So she accepted the tea and moved with Dean to the couch, where a pillow and blanket were arranged.

His laptop and phone lay on the coffee table beside a notepad and pen. The dark video of cars in the park's small lot centered the screen.

She curled her feet beneath her, balancing the hot drink in her hands. "How do you do it?" she asked. "How do you keep going to work, performing the same job that nearly killed you? It's been more than a year since you found that boy's body, and it still haunts you. It will probably always haunt you, but you keep going."

"His name was Ben Smothers," Dean said, voice low and fighting emotion. He peered at her with tortured eyes as he lowered to the cushion at her side. "I keep going because what I do matters, and I help everyone I can. Ben was an exception, and to stop helping others because I was too late to help him doesn't make any logical sense. So I keep going, even when I don't want to, and even if I'm not sure I can make the kind of difference I hope.

"And I didn't find Ben's body. I found him. Hanging on to life by a thread. I carried him half a mile through the woods to my truck, and I drove him six miles until I found cell service, all while listening to his rattled, shallow breaths and begging the universe to keep his heart beating until I got help." He swallowed, and his cheeks darkened. "The universe declined."

Nicole's breath caught. "Dean."

He lifted a palm to stop her, jaw clenching and releasing.

She hadn't known the boy had been alive for a second of his time with him. "You never told me."

"I needed time. And you left me."

The verbal blow knocked the wind from her lungs. She'd given him three months to open up and let her back in. When he didn't, she walked out, clinging to the insistence she deserved a partner, and calling it quits because he'd fallen short of his promise on that front. In hindsight, she could see she'd really left because she was exhausted from always being the strong one for others in trauma. She'd left to protect her tired, battered heart, the same way her mom had left their dad, pulling away long before he'd asked for a divorce.

And Nicole had blamed Dean.

"I wasn't trying to push you away," he said. "I was trying to hold myself together."

She set her hand on his, bracing for the rejection she deserved. She'd stood by her sister through endless self-inflicted misery and poor choices, but when the man she'd planned to marry withdrew to process an unthinkable trauma, she'd dumped him. "I'm so sorry."

He offered a small, sad smile. "Me, too."

"I was scared, and I ran," she admitted. "But at the time, I didn't know that's what I was doing."

The floodgates opened, and truth flowed freely from her heart to her lips. Dean accepted her words, then shared his own. He confided in her about his experience on the Ben Smothers case and about the counseling he'd received afterward. Nicole confessed her fears of never being enough.

Time passed in strange lulls and spurts as they

spoke, and she begged the night to last forever. She wasn't ready for Blakely to wake and need her, for another day of Cari's absence, or for these moments of raw honesty to end.

Dean turned his palm beneath hers, twining their fingers and tugging her close.

She set the long-empty cup of tea onto the coffee table and climbed into his lap like a child, wrapping her arms around his neck and melting into him.

Dean searched her with careful blue eyes. Then he lifted a wide, warm palm to cradle her jaw.

She leaned into the touch, and he released a ragged breath in response.

Then he lowered his gaze to her lips and kissed her. Chaste and sweet, the gesture filled her heart with hope and her mind with peace.

She rested her head against his chest and drifted back to sleep, cursing her relentless fatigue.

She woke in his arms a short while later, as the first rays of sun climbed the windowsills.

Their long-overdue talk had changed everything for her, as had their kiss. She could only hope he felt the same by light of day.

"Hope." The word formed on her lips and opened her eyes.

"What?" Dean looked at her, already awake.

She pushed away, setting herself upright, mind racing and hope blooming anew. "I think I know the password to Cari's phone."

Dean grabbed his phone from the coffee table and

dialed. He pressed Send, then accessed the speaker option and poised the phone between them.

"Hey, Dean," Finn answered on a yawn. "What's up?"

"I'm here with Nicole," Dean said. "You're on speaker."

"Okay," he said slowly. "What's going on?"

"Do you have Cari's cell phone?" Nicole asked. "Is it already at the lab?"

"I dropped it off last night, why?"

"I think I know the password."

Something shifted on Finn's end of the line. "Hang on. I fell asleep at the station. I'm texting the lab now to see if anyone's there. What time is it?" He groaned, apparently answering his own question. "Oh. I've got a response. Kim's already at work. Let me catch her up."

Nicole wet her lips and looked to Dean, willing her idea to be right. "Tell her to try the password NEWHOPE, use the numbers on the keypad. No spaces or symbols or anything."

"Yeah," Finn said. "Give me a sec."

Nicole's knee bobbed. "Be right," she whispered. "Be right. Be right. Be right."

Several long moments passed, and Nicole chewed her lip in anticipation.

"That worked," Finn said. "Nice job."

Dean pressed a kiss to her forehead, as if it was the most natural thing in the world, and her heart thudded with joy. "What now?" he asked Finn, eyes fixed on Nicole.

"I'm already halfway to the lab," he said.

"Now you can log Cari out of her social media and email accounts," Nicole said. "Stop whoever took her laptop from accessing anything useful." In case they made it past her lock screen.

Sounds of a buzzer and the opening and closing of doors came through the phone line, then Finn's voice, declaring himself and requesting to speak with someone named Kim.

"On it," he said a moment later. "First I need to make notes of everyone she's been in recent contact with and capture screenshots of their communication."

"Can you send some of that to us?" Nicole asked. "Maybe I'll recognize someone's name."

"Sure," Finn said. "Give me twenty minutes to get going on this, and I'll send some texts."

Her smile grew. "Thank you."

Dean disconnected the call and returned the phone to the coffee table. He peeled himself from the sofa and headed to the kitchen. "New hope, huh?"

"She learned that at the ranch." Excitement and possibility churned in Nicole's core. "Every decision is a new chance to change your life."

The moment felt pivotal. Cari's case was no longer a complete dead end. They had access to a whole phone full of leads, and Nicole nearly vibrated with the need to get started.

As if on cue, Dean's phone dinged with a new text message. It dinged again before he could return from the kitchen and unlock the screen. A third image appeared as he raised it into view of them both. Finn was sending screenshots from Cari's phone log. Then a message.

Finn: Does Nicole recognize any of these names?

Nicole scanned the names and numbers, then shook her head.

Dean: No

Finn: I'm getting called to a scene. I'll be in touch soon.

Adrenaline coursed through Nicole's chest and limbs. She wouldn't need caffeine to get her moving today. She felt ready to burst. "I'm going to call the numbers."

Dean frowned. "Maybe Finn should handle that."

Nicole bristled. "Why?" He was leaving on a case. Who knew when he'd have time to do the research needed. "I can do it. Take notes. Report back. He went on a call. I'm not doing anything."

"What happens if Cari's contacts don't want to talk to you? What if they don't realize there's a problem yet, and you cause one by alerting them to her disappearance? Then they don't answer the phone when Finn calls?"

She considered that a moment. He was right, of course, and she needed to think this through. But time was also of the essence.

Eventually, they agreed on calling Finn, both to

ask permission and to request he get Kim from the crime lab to chat with them. A few minutes later, Nicole was on the line with Kim, who dialed Cari's most frequent contact using three-way calling from Cari's phone.

"Ready?" Kim asked.

"I think so."

"Okay. I'm going to start the recording, then dial Darla D."

Blakely's small voice rose from the guest room in a series of fussing sounds, and Dean moved in that direction while the call connected.

"Cari!" A woman's shrill voice burst through the line before the first ring was complete. "Oh my goodness. Are you okay? I can't believe this. What is happening? I've been freaking terrified," she ranted, sounding out of breath and possibly near tears. "Someone said you took that last job and then vanished. I've been asking everyone where you are, but no one knew. I thought you were dead. Wait. Do you need help? I can get you on my way to work. You can take my car after that if you need it. Where are you?"

"Uhm," Nicole began, unsure what to say to the woman's pure panic. A torrent of emotion choked her words.

"The newspaper said one of the party guests was killed in a robbery," she whispered. "But that's not what the girls are saying. Is that why you're gone? Do you know what really happened?"

"Who's dead?" Nicole asked, the word squeaking out before she thought better of it. Why hadn't the police realized there was a possible murder in town or that it might be related to Cari's disappearance?

"Dr. George. Cari?"

"Mmm-hmm."

Darla was quiet. "Who is this?"

Nicole debated lying, pretending to be Cari, anything to keep her on the line, but she was stuck. Darla could hang up at any moment and choose not to answer again. "I'm Cari's sister," she confessed, speaking as rapidly as Darla had a moment before. "I can't find her. I'm watching her baby, and I'm scared. I don't know what to do or who to call. You were the person she spoke to most. Please help me."

Silence returned, gonging across the line.

"Please," she begged. "I have no one else to ask. I don't understand what's happening, and I need to find her. Anything you share could make the difference in whether or not Cari comes home. I swear I won't tell anyone what you say."

The silence continued so long Nicole pulled the phone from her ear to be sure the call hadn't been dropped.

"I work at Nina's Boutique on Seacrest Avenue," Darla said, tone flat and resigned. "I'll be there all day. You can stop in, but don't act like you know me, make sure you weren't followed, and never call back. You're putting me in danger."

"She's gone," Kim said a few seconds later. "Let me know if you need anything else."

"Thanks." Nicole tucked the phone into her pocket.

Dean exited the guest room with Blakely in tow. "How'd it go?"

"Better than expected," she said. "We need to eat and get dressed. We're going shopping."

Chapter Fourteen

Dean cleaned up breakfast while the ladies took their showers and got ready for the day. So many things had happened in the last twelve hours, he wasn't sure how to feel or what to process first, but with a new lead on Cari's case, it was definitely time to hustle, so he chose to concentrate on that.

Except, even as he wiped down Blakely's high chair and loaded dishes into the dishwasher, his night with Nicole danced back through his mind. They'd finally talked the way they should have more than a year ago.

And he'd kissed her.

He hadn't intended to go for it. Hadn't meant to lose himself in the moment. It was completely inappropriate, not to mention unprofessional, of him to make a move on her, given her current emotional state and general situation. But he had.

And she'd kissed him back.

His lips twisted into a self-indulgent smile.

He'd slept better with her in his arms for a few hours than he had in months. Maybe a year. Now Finn

had access to Cari's phone, and her friend Darla had
agreed to meet them. It was a darn good day. The possibility of finding Cari seemed closer than it had since
the moment he'd learned she was missing.

A thunderous rap on his front door sent a curse
from his lips.

He dried his hands on a dish towel, glancing toward
the closed bathroom door before picking up his sidearm and moving to the front window.

Austin's truck was in the driveway. Austin was
on the porch.

Dean opened the door, and his brother scanned him,
taking notice of the hand kept out of sight.

"Hey now," Austin said, a cocky grin sliding into
place. "You planning on shooting me?"

"Maybe." Dean put the gun away and headed for
the kitchen. "Why are you pounding on the door like
you're here to serve a warrant?"

"I wanted you to hear me. In case you were sleeping." He stepped over the threshold and shut the door.
"Where are the girls? They finally get sick of you and
leave? Decide to take their chances back at the apartment?"

Dean glanced over his shoulder. "Funny. Keep it up
and maybe I will shoot you."

Austin grinned. "I come in peace, big brother, and
bearing news."

"In that case, I have coffee." He motioned to the
table, and Austin sat.

"I found a cooperative old lady in that fancy neighborhood. She invited me in for herbal tea and those little shortbread cookies with jam in the middle."

Dean laughed, despite himself. "I knew you'd change your mind about dating eventually."

"If I was fifty years older, Myrtle wouldn't be able to get rid of me," Austin said. "Her son's a gem, too. He worries about her, so he installed cameras all around her property. The good ones. Not the cheap stuff. She let me take a look at the footage from the night of the party."

The bathroom door opened, and Nicole appeared with Blakely on her hip. "Wait," she said, hurrying into view with a towel wrapped around her hair. "Hey, Austin. I was eavesdropping while I got this one ready." She lifted Blakely in front of her and blew against her round tummy, then cuddled her close.

Blakely squealed in delight. Her brown curls were pulled into one tiny fountain of a ponytail at the top of her head. And she wore a two-piece shorts set with a tank top. Both were yellow and covered in butterflies.

Nicole had faded jeans on with small rips and holes on the knees and thighs. Her off-white T-shirt emphasized her tan. "What did I miss?"

Dean did his best not to admire the long curve of her neck or think about sliding his fingers into the slick wet curls beneath her towel.

Instead, he motioned to his brother. "Austin convinced an old lady to give him sugar and let him see her cameras."

She wrinkled her nose. "Well, I'm glad you decided to date again."

Dean barked a laugh.

Austin made a disgruntled face. "Myrtle caught the Tippins' home and the side street to the park on those cameras. Do you want to see the footage or keep poking at me?"

Nicole slid her eyes to Dean and mouthed the word *Myrtle*.

Austin withdrew his phone from a pocket and turned it to face them. An image of the Tippins' home and driveway appeared. "What's the first thing you notice?"

"A ton of cars," Nicole said, drawn to the screen like a moth to light. "And they're all really nice. I'm just going by the emblems, but I'm pretty sure I can't even afford to think about most of these cars."

She was right.

Dean took a moment to appreciate the number of luxury vehicles. Based on the rides alone, partygoers were clearly wealthy, or at least driving cars only wealthy people could afford. Sadly, the people were too distant and pixilated to identify based on the video alone.

"This goes on for thirty-five minutes," Austin said. "Expensive cars pull up, fancy people get out, a valet drives the car away. Next car arrives. Repeat."

"Have you shown this to Finn?" Dean asked.

"Yep. He's got someone at the station running the plates on these cars." He pointed to a car being moved by the valet; it drove toward the camera before turning at the next crossroad. When he tapped the screen to stop the video, a partial plate was visible in the night. "He'll ID as many owners as possible, then give them all a call. Now, look at this." He turned the phone toward him a moment before facing the screen in their direction again. "Twenty minutes before all that, this happens."

A large panel van, like the kind that picks people up from airports, pulled into the Tippins' driveway. A dozen women in black dresses climbed out.

Cari was one of them.

Nicole covered her mouth, then fell onto a chair. Blakely made a swipe for the phone.

Austin backed it up a few inches. He froze the frame. "She's wearing that lavender jacket. And carrying her phone in this image, so we know she made it to the party, then gave up those items later."

Dean rubbed his stubbled cheek. "An all-female catering company?" All young and beautiful.

"All wearing slinky black dresses and heels," Austin added. "You know what they don't have with them? Food."

Nicole's gaze drifted to Austin, then Dean. She held Blakely a little more closely. "Maybe the food and drinks were delivered earlier. Cari can't cook. She was only there to serve."

Austin shot Dean a look, then tucked away his phone. "Finn's headed to the car dealership where Mr. Tippin works," he said, avoiding Nicole's suggestion. "He's hoping to rattle him by showing up there, maybe get some more information from him, talk to his coworkers. I'm still looking for Mikey. Something tells me he's the key to finding whoever schedules these parties, and I'm willing to bet that person will know everything else we're looking to learn."

"Mikey's still gone?" Nicole asked.

"He's probably just lying low," Austin said. "And guys like him could probably get into the back seat of a cruiser without most members of the force even knowing."

"What makes you think you can find him?"

Austin tapped his nose. "I'm a bloodhound." He stood and rounded the table to kiss Nicole's cheek, then Blakely's head. "Let me know if you learn anything else, or if Finn calls you before me. Something's definitely fishy in suburbia. It's been a long while since Marshal's Bluff had an illegal ring of some kind."

Dean followed him to the door. "Thanks for coming by with the footage." Knowing they were another step closer to finding Cari would be great for Nicole's spirits.

"Don't mention it." Austin opened the door, then paused on the threshold. "What do you think is going on?" he asked in a voice intended only for Dean. "Gambling? Smuggling? Drugs?" He mouthed the word *prostitution*.

"I can read lips," Nicole said.

Austin winced and lifted a palm in apology. "Why can she read lips?" he whispered.

"I teach second graders," she answered, not giving Dean a chance to guess.

"Half the kids refuse to speak loudly enough to be heard, and the other half are continually scheming for extra playtime or snacks. Or plotting unfunny pranks. I learned to pay attention. My sister isn't a prostitute."

Austin had the decency to look ashamed. "I wasn't suggesting she—" He cleared his throat. "I'm just spitballing ideas. Knowing what we're dealing with will help us know whose doors to knock on. No offense intended. I swear."

"Fine, but hold on." She shoved away from the table and came to a stop at Dean's side. "I spoke with one of Cari's contacts this morning. We gained access to her phone, and a tech at the station helped us connect with a woman named Darla."

He pulled his lips down and shot his eyebrows high. "Nice work."

"Thanks. Have you heard about a recent murder? Someone named Dr. George. The papers said it was a robbery?"

He frowned. "No, but I've been busy with this case since you told us about Cari."

"See what you can find out?" Dean asked.

"Sure, but have you tried the internet for local news?"

"Not yet," Nicole said. "We just learned about Dr. George, and we've been trying to get out of here to meet with Darla since I hung up with her."

Austin clasped his hands and kneaded them. "All right. Sounds like we've all got our missions today. Let's go bring our girl home."

"Deal," she said.

He jogged down the steps and climbed into his waiting truck.

Dean turned to Nicole with an apologetic smile. He wished Austin hadn't mentioned prostitution, but he was thankful to be there for her, if she'd let him. "You okay?"

She fell against him in a gentle embrace, cradling Blakely between them.

"Things are starting to move," he said. "It can feel like a lot, but it's all good."

"I know."

Dean's phone dinged, and Finn's number appeared on-screen.

"Austin's truck slowed at the end of the driveway," Nicole said, reaching for the sheer curtain.

Either he was stopping to send the message, or the brothers were receiving a group text.

He swiped his thumb across the screen to reveal the message. "Group text."

Nicole angled her head for a better look at the words.

Finn: Mikey was discovered behind the pizzeria this morning. Beaten nearly unrecognizable.

Finn: Going with him to the hospital now.

Dean didn't respond. Shock coiled in him, and he looked outside to see how Austin was taking the news.

His truck's brake lights went out, and the vehicle rolled away.

Nicole sighed deeply, regaining his attention and apparently her resolve. "Let's stop at Ricky Rocket's on the way to meet Darla. She's going to be at work all day, and I don't know how long the woman who found Mikey will be at the pizzeria."

Dean pulled his keys from the rack. "All right, but this time we're taking my truck."

Chapter Fifteen

Nicole carried Blakely in her sling as they walked along the quaint downtown sidewalk toward the pizzeria. Shoppers were out in the usual summertime droves, carrying handled bags of newfound treasures and sipping iced drinks from logoed cups with straws. The morning was balmy and overcast as the sun worked to burn away the clouds, but Nicole felt more hopeful and invigorated than hot or worried.

Blakely cooed contentedly against her, happy to be outside and in her sling, enjoying the sights, scents and sounds.

Dean stepped forward to open the door to Ricky Rocket's when they arrived.

It was still early, and the air inside smelled of coffee and something sweet. Patrons claimed a few tables near the window. Mini pizzas topped with cinnamon sugar and icing positioned before them.

Nicole moved toward the counter, Dean's hand against her back. The restaurant's interior looked the same as it had before, but unlike her last visit, the tension inside was thick. No chatter or laughter rose from the kitchen, only the sounds of running water and the occasional clang of trays against the counter.

The expression on the cashier's face was brittle but pleasant. Her lips parted as recognition dawned.

Dean opened his wallet immediately. "Two bottles of water."

She nodded, and Nicole offered a small smile.

"Can we talk for a minute?" Nicole asked softly as Laney rang up the water. "We were here looking for Mikey earlier this week. You might remember."

Laney nodded but didn't make eye contact.

"You probably heard about what happened to me that day," Nicole said. "Maybe your boss or Detective Beaumont explained our story?"

Laney gave Dean the water and a register total, then took his money. "Your sister is missing." She made change, glancing briefly at Blakely. "The baby's mom."

"That's right." The answer came easier than it had before, and Nicole hated everything that fact implied. Her mind had accepted this as reality. Her sister was missing, and that was the new normal. "This is Blakely," she said, stroking her niece's cheek beneath the eyelet sunbonnet. "My sister and Mikey are friends, and he's introduced her to some catering jobs in the evenings. She went missing from one of those assignments. We think Mikey knows who hired her and how we can get in touch with them."

The younger woman's lips parted, and her eyes widened. She scanned the dining area, then looked toward the kitchen.

"If you know something, you can tell us," Nicole

said. "This is Dean Beaumont. He's a private investigator and a friend of mine and my sister's. He's Detective Beaumont's brother."

Laney looked at Dean, uncertain.

"Please. We need to find her before she's hurt or... worse." Her mouth dried with the utterance, unable to comprehend a world without her sister in it.

"I found him today," Laney said. "I work the first shift, and when I got here, he was just lying outside the door. I didn't even recognize him. His face was so destroyed. His clothes were filthy. I thought he didn't have a home and maybe he'd slept there intentionally last night. Then I noticed Mikey's car in the lot. Mikey's never here in the morning. Then I recognized his shoes." Her eyes brimmed with tears, and she blinked them back, breathless. "He didn't respond when I called out to him or when I shook him. I thought he was dead. I couldn't find a pulse. It looks easy on TV, but it's not. I was shaking and my ears were ringing. I called 911 and just sat there waiting to know if he was alive."

"You did well," Dean said, pulling the woman's eyes to his. "You acted quickly and got help. Your actions likely saved his life."

She covered her mouth with both hands, and the tears began to fall.

Laney requested her fifteen-minute break and led Nicole and Dean to a small room in the back.

They sat at a folding lunch table with mismatched chairs and watched as Laney fidgeted with a straw wrapper someone had left behind.

"Mikey always wanted to make the deliveries to the rich neighborhoods," she began. "He said they tipped better. The other drivers thought the rich people were terrible tippers, and the neighborhoods were too far away, which limited the number of deliveries they could make. So it all worked out. One night when we were closing up, Mikey told me a customer gave him a business card and invited him to be a server at a fancy party. Afterward, he said they paid him in cash for the work, plus he made good tips and the homes were like nothing he'd ever experienced. Too fancy for words."

Dean shifted forward, resting his forearms on the table. "Did he mention the customer's name?"

"No, but he called the company Rising Tides. It sounded too easy to me. Too good to be true, and that usually means sketchy. Mikey thought you were one of the rich guys from the company."

Nicole fought a smile. Dean's brothers liked to tease him for being a little higher maintenance than they were. For using product on his beard every fall. For knowing the difference between Carhartt and Calvin Klein and for wearing less of the former than the latter.

Dean slid his eyes in her direction before returning them to Laney.

"That's why he ran," she said. "He called me later to let me know he was okay."

"Did he tell you anything else?" Dean asked. "Anything you remember will help."

Laney gave a humorless smile. "Mikey was always

recruiting, looking for more women to serve at parties. He said the candidates had to be young and clean up nice. They also needed to keep their mouths shut, but he swore the pay was worth it. He tried to get me to go to meetings where he claimed additional information would be provided. I got the impression those meetings were interviews that gave the higher-ups a chance to choose who they wanted. The whole thing icked me out. Until I graduate and the student loans come due, I make enough here to get by."

"Do you still have that address?"

"I think." Laney scrolled through her phone.

"Did you tell Detective Beaumont all this?" he asked.

She pressed her lips together, looking sheepish. "No. I didn't know this was relevant. I was shocked by the guy holding a knife to you," she said, addressing Nicole. "He stabbed you when you had a baby in your arms. Who does that? I needed time." She passed her phone to Dean. "This is it, but you didn't get it from me."

He accepted the device, then removed his phone from his pocket.

"I don't know what Mikey told whoever beat him, but from the condition he was in, he probably confessed it all. Whatever that is. I don't think I would've survived it. I don't want to find out. You know what I'm saying?"

"Of course," Nicole agreed. Laney had been smart enough to stay out of all this. She didn't want to drag her into it now, when she was willing to try to help.

Dean took a photo of Laney's screen, presumably to avoid evidence of Laney's communication with him. For her protection.

Nicole kissed Blakely's head, the reality of Cari's situation becoming clearer. All those wealthy people had arrived in fancy cars. And one of them was using Rising Tides as a way to take advantage of young people in need of easy money. Maybe even exploiting those same people. Because who would believe Mikey or Cari over the supreme elite?

She nearly laughed at the pretention and naive presumption. Obviously anyone running on that mindset had never met her sister, or experienced the Beaumont family on a mission.

Someone somewhere was about to get an education.

DEAN BEEPED THE doors to his truck unlocked, then opened the passenger side for Nicole. He helped her remove Blakely from the sling, then tucked her into her car seat in the extended cab. Nicole seemed to be in less pain today, which was a good sign of healing and a massive weight off his chest.

Once everyone was buckled in safely, he took a beat to mentally explode over the audacity of some rich locals taking advantage of struggling youths. Why were so many people absolutely awful?

"Thinking about this company, Rising Tides?" Nicole asked. "And how they intentionally drew young people in and exploited their need for money?"

He blew out a breath. "Yep."

She stroked a gentle hand down his arm, pulling his gaze to meet hers. "I've only been following you around for a few days, so I'm not saying I know what it's like to be you, but I think I'm beginning to understand the toll a job like this could take on someone."

He frowned, unsure where this was going.

"Before this week, I'd only seen the bits you showed me. The victories. The joy of a tough case closed. Families reunited. Bad guys busted."

He dipped his chin, wondering if she was about to pass judgment. Maybe point out something he could do better. And he knew there was plenty of room for corrections. This week had been a trial on every level. He normally worked alone. He never had to do his job while trying to keep someone else safe, definitely not two people, never a baby. Normally, it didn't feel as if the whole world was waiting for him to fulfill his promise to bring someone home safely. "It's not usually like this," he said, preparing his defense.

He started the engine and unlocked his cell phone. It was time to go. Check out the address Laney had given them. This conversation could wait.

"I should've been more patient with you before we broke up," she said.

"What?" Dean turned back to face her, chest tightening. That hadn't been the blow he'd anticipated.

"I didn't see the whole picture," she said. "I was focused on myself when I should've been focused on you, and that wasn't fair. You're always thinking of everyone else, and I let you down. I'm really sorry."

His heart swelled, relieved and grateful for words

he didn't realize he'd needed to hear. They'd spoken at length the night before, but this confession meant everything. He unfastened his seat belt and reached for her, emotion tugging at his heart and squeezing his lungs.

She smiled as he closed the distance and kissed her. Her lips were soft and yielding; they parted easily as she slanted her mouth to his. Last night's kiss had been chaste and accepting, a seal on all their shared confessions. This kiss tasted like dreams and promises.

This was how things were meant to be. Him and her. Facing things together.

He longed to take her straight home. He wanted to tangle his body with hers and lose himself in her for days. Until life forced them up for air.

Blakely babbled, then squealed behind them, and Nicole broke the kiss with a laugh.

Her fingers curled against the back of his neck, tracing the hairline. She released him reluctantly, and he righted himself behind the wheel.

Unable to erase the goofy smile on his face, he focused on his phone screen. "Let's get this address plugged into the truck's GPS, then I'll forward it on to Finn. We can do a quick drive-by to check the place out before we go see Darla."

"Is Finn still at the hospital with Mikey?"

"Probably not," Dean said, checking the time on his watch. "There wouldn't have been much to do there. I'm guessing he's at the car dealership questioning Mr. Tippin by now, unless something else came up."

He tapped the address into the display on the truck's dashboard and waited while the navigation system set a course.

The street grid zoomed and turned, setting a blue arrow to represent their current location and a red pin at their destination. The ocean took up half the screen. "Looks like we're headed for the coast." But not the rougher, industrial part of town. They were going to the section of Marshal's Bluff that looked like downtown, but every price tag had an extra zero. An area Dean sadly frequented during divorce and cheating-spouse cases.

He supposed that made perfect sense.

"Dean," Nicole said, leaning forward and extending a finger toward the navigation's display. "That's the car dealership."

Chapter Sixteen

Finn was on his phone outside the dealership when Dean pulled into a space beside a pair of cruisers.

"Wow." Nicole unfastened her seat belt, gaze fixed on the scene outside. "Two cruisers and a detective. Were they all here before we called?"

"Must've been," Dean said. It'd only taken them a few minutes to make the trip from Ricky Rocket's. He doubted the officers could've beaten them, unless they'd already been en route.

He settled the truck's engine and climbed out, taking a beat to make silly faces at Blakely, before freeing her from the car seat.

Nicole appeared at his side, her sling in place around her shoulder. "I've got her," she said, opening the fabric for Dean to tuck in the baby.

Finn approached next, his cell phone out of sight. "Mr. Tippin wasn't at his home when I paid a visit, and according to his employees and coworkers, he hasn't shown up here, either," he said. "Given the way this case seems to continually circle back to him, I'm going to assume the cause of Mr. Tippin's absence is

directly related to Mike Litchfield's assault, and he's
lying low."

"That sounds about right," Dean said. "Why the
extra men? You find something?"

Finn looked toward the building, its floor-to-ceiling
windows at least thirty feet high. Several vehicles inside were arranged in a semicircle while others were
elevated on pedestals at different heights.

"As it turns out," Finn said, "several of the cars
caught on that video Austin tracked down were pur-
chased here. Most were sold by Mr. Tippin."

Nicole rocked gently as she stood at Dean's side.
"What does that mean?"

It was a good question, one Dean had been puz-
zling through as well.

"We don't know yet," Finn said. "That's what we're
here to find out. Come on inside." He moved slowly
toward the building, speaking as he walked. "We're
trying not to disrupt the business day more than necessary, assuming Mr. Tippin acted alone. Though to
be honest, all these people are suspects until I can
figure out who was or wasn't involved."

Dean passed his brother and grabbed the door for
them to enter.

Men in suits and women in heels gathered at desks,
watching the officers interview their coworkers. A
couple with a double stroller peeked inside a giant
SUV, discussing the benefits of style over the practicality of a minivan.

Framed photos of the staff lined a wall outside a
series of offices overlooking the sales floor.

Nicole stopped beside Mr. Tippin's photo and turned to stare.

"That's him?" Dean asked.

"Yeah."

The man was in his late forties in the photo, dressed in a suit and wearing a charismatic smile.

Finn knocked lightly on the wall and angled his head toward the nearest office, directing them inside. "We're waiting for a judge to provide a search warrant so we can get a look at company files. Right now our evidence of Tippin's involvement is circumstantial, but we're trying to change that."

"Did you run a background check?" Dean asked.

Finn frowned. "Obviously."

"And?"

"Cleaner than half the Beaumont brothers."

Nicole chuckled, and Dean smiled, despite himself. He and his brothers hadn't always been who they were now.

"No priors," Finn continued. "Not even a traffic ticket. He and his wife are model citizens on paper."

Nicole stepped away from the brothers, always in motion when Blakely was in her care. She made a circuit through the room, looking carefully at each framed photo on the desk and bookshelves. "Any idea who runs Rising Tides, or if that's even a real company?"

"No, and it's not registered with the North Carolina business bureau," he said. "That's as far as I got, but it's on today's agenda."

"What about the death?" Dean asked. He'd given

Finn a complete rundown of their talk with Laney on their ride over. He didn't expect his brother to have answers yet, but the question was still worth asking. If Finn needed extra hands or eyes, Austin could step in.

"That's interesting," Finn said. "I reached out to the officer who made the initial report on the body and crime scene. I was on the line with her when you arrived. An older male doctor named George Maline was found inside his car with a deadly amount of painkillers in his system. His wallet was emptied, but his Rolex was still on his wrist. And the car was worth more than my annual salary. I don't know how much cash had been inside his wallet, but I'm guessing the watch and car were of higher value."

Dean bobbed his head. "Staged robbery."

"That's my guess," Finn concurred. "Though initially it was seen as an overdose. An autopsy indicated habitual use of the same prescription."

"An addict," Nicole said. She'd heard of doctors getting hooked on pills and writing themselves prescriptions to keep the medication coming.

Finn nodded.

A female officer appeared in the doorway. "Detective?"

Finn lifted his chin in acknowledgment. "On my way."

The officer left, and Finn offered Dean a fist bump before waving goodbye to Nicole and Blakely. "Stay in touch," he said.

"Back at ya," Dean echoed.

HALF AN HOUR LATER, Nicole climbed down from Dean's truck for the third time in less than three hours, feeling the stretch and burn of her healing side, and the minor exertion of carrying Blakely in a sling all morning. The possibility of finding her sister felt closer than ever before, and she couldn't bring herself to ask for a break. She and Dean had stopped for smoothies after visiting the car dealership, so she could change Blakely and give herself a little boost.

"How are you doing?" Dean asked, beeping the truck doors locked and meeting Nicole outside Nina's, a small clothing and jewelry boutique near the bay.

The lot was full of mostly fancy cars, and the traffic predictably heavy given the season and perfect southern summer weather.

"I'm getting nervous," she admitted. "I don't want Darla to change her mind about speaking with us, and part of me wonders if she's really in there, or if she just said she would be to get us off the phone."

Dean slid an arm around her shoulders, tucking her against his side and dropping a kiss on her head. "Whatever happens, whoever's in there, or isn't, we've got this."

She exhaled a load of unwarranted panic. "Okay."

"Finn's following leads in a bunch of directions now. Anything we learn from Darla is going to be icing, but it's not the cake."

Nicole nodded, and they began to move.

Dean's arm loosened around her, but he kept a hand on her lower back, maintaining physical contact. "Remember not to ask for her," he said. "She doesn't want us to let on that we know her. She must think she's being watched."

He opened the etched-glass door, then followed her into the air-conditioned shop.

Racks of pastel tops and floral dresses were gathered around a table featuring straw hats, beach bags and flip-flops. Similar displays fanned out in both directions, showcasing jewelry, novelty items and socks. Headless mannequins on tabletops were dressed for a night on the town.

An exit sign hung over a hallway on the back wall, beside a small checkout counter and fitting rooms. A petite redhead folded clothes near the register, eyes darting repeatedly toward the front door.

"Welcome to Nina's," she said, tracking Nicole and Dean with her gaze. "Anything I can help you with?"

Nicole searched for the right words to identify herself without causing trouble, unsure the woman at the counter was even the one she'd come to talk to. "I'm looking for something for my sister," she said. "I brought her daughter to help me."

The woman stilled. She scanned the empty shop, then lifted one of the tops she'd been folding. "What do you think of this?"

"Cute."

"Is your sister your size? I can set you up in a fitting room. You can try it on and see what you think."

Dean reached for Blakely. "Why don't I hold the princess while you do that?"

Nicole nodded anxiously, freeing her niece from the sling, then unhooking the material from around her shoulders and passing that to Dean as well. "Thanks."

Dean nodded toward the dressing rooms, and she moved slowly in the redhead's direction, feeling strangely uncertain, as if this might be a trap.

A tall blonde in platform sandals dragged a rolling rack from the hallway beneath the exit sign. She smiled at Nicole. "Finding everything okay?"

Nicole nodded. "Yep. Thank you." She stopped at the counter and selected an olive-green tank top from the stack. "May I try this one?"

The redhead straightened, a pile of similar tops strewn over one forearm. "Sure." She headed for the dressing rooms, and Nicole followed.

Her oval black name tag contained a single word in gold script letters.

Darla.

She knocked on a fitting room, then unlocked it and held the door for Nicole. "If you like that one, we carry it in multiple colors. Blue and red are both popular." She removed the top two shirts from the pile on her arm and handed them to Nicole. "Let me know if I can get you anything else or if you need a different size."

She stepped out, and the door swung shut, leaving Nicole alone in the wooden cube.

"I think you'll like the red one," Darla said, her voice projecting into the little room.

Nicole raised the item in question, and a slip of paper floated out, drifting to a stop on the bench beside a full-length mirror. "I'm trying it now," she said.

Her heartbeat raced as she collected and unfolded the paper. Her hands trembled as she read the words.

Destroy this message. Buy one of these shirts. Meet me out back.

Nicole tore the paper into bits and shoved them into her pocket, then gathered the tank tops and let herself out.

Dean leaned against the wall outside the fitting room, waiting.

"I'm going to get this tank top," Nicole said, heading to the counter. She set the green and blue options aside and pushed the red one toward the register.

The blonde met her with a smile. "Just the one?"

"Yes, please."

Nicole paid, glancing repeatedly at Darla, who didn't make eye contact again. Then she followed Dean out, passing the redhead without further comment.

Back inside the truck, he looked to Nicole, brows high. "What happened in the fitting room?"

She pulled her sunglasses from the cup holder and slid them over her eyes, still shaky from the bizarre encounter. "She gave me a note. We're supposed to meet her out back."

His lips quirked slightly as he started the engine. "Nice work."

"If I haven't expressed it before," Nicole said, voice wobbly, "I am not cut out for this. I don't know how you stay cool all the time. I'm a wreck, and nothing even happened in there. The most intense situation I can handle on a daily basis is a classroom full of eight-year-olds."

Dean grimaced. "I wouldn't survive a day like that."

She smiled as he piloted the big truck through the crowded lot and into a small alley behind the retail establishments. The lane was probably only accessed by delivery trucks and trash collectors with any kind of regularity.

He parked near a dumpster and cut the engine.

Nicole stared at the back door to Nina's, waiting for Darla to appear.

Minutes ticked by, and she didn't show.

Nicole fixed a bottle for Blakely, then watched the clock as the baby drank.

Fifteen minutes passed.

Then twenty.

Dean scanned the area on a slow visual circuit. "She might have to wait for a scheduled break."

"Then why didn't she tell me when that was?"

"She was scared," he said. "Probably not thinking clearly. I could see her uncertainly in every movement from across the store. Fidgeting, darting gaze, rushed speech. A preoccupation with the front door, as if she suspected she was being watched."

Nicole's skin crawled. "You think she was being watched?"

"I didn't see anyone, but the lot's full and traffic's heavy," he said. "My main focus was on you. As for Darla, I think she wants to talk or she wouldn't have asked us to wait out here, so as long as you and Blakely are comfortable, I say we—"

The back door to Nina's opened and Darla appeared with a small bag of trash.

Dean climbed out and closed the truck door with a barely audible click.

Nicole rushed to do the same.

Blakely was asleep and stayed that way as Nicole moved her from the car seat to the sling.

She met Dean at the truck's grille.

Darla was frozen near the dumpster, the small bag dangling from her fingertips.

"Do we approach her?" Nicole asked.

"No."

"What if she changes her mind?"

"She's come this far," he said. "Let's be patient a little longer and see what happens."

Nicole chewed her lip, knowing he was right, even if the need to act pulsed wildly through her veins.

Darla shook her head a few times, then tossed the trash into a dumpster and started moving toward the truck, a look of resolve on her thin face. "I only have a minute," she said quickly, "so I'm going to talk. You can listen, but you can't come back here or call me again."

Nicole nodded, biting her tongue to stop the tidal wave of questions.

"I'm leaving work early. I told my boss I'm sick, which isn't a complete lie. I don't know where Cari is." Her voice cracked, and her expression crumpled into distress. "I have to work a party tonight and pretend as if everything is fine so no one suspects I'm ready to crack. Dr. George is dead and my friend is missing. Things are definitely not fine, and I don't know what to do."

Dean opened his wallet and offered her a business card.

She took it. "What's this?"

"It's a ranch outside town that helps people in need and provides a place to stay while folks get through tough times. The people there will help you. They can keep you safe."

She wrapped her arms around her middle, clutching the card in one hand. "I have to keep up appearances. I think they're watching me. They know I was close with Cari and probably suspect I'll go to the police, file a report and tell them where she worked last."

"We've already done all that," Nicole said.

Darla's eyes widened. "This is why they look for people without family ties. If something goes wrong, they can keep us quiet, but not outsiders, cause y'all don't get it."

"Get what?" Nicole asked, forgetting her orders to be quiet and listen.

Darla rolled her eyes and shook her head again. "I've got to go."

"Wait! We asked about Dr. George," Nicole said.

She paused. "Was it murder?"

Dean nodded. "That's what it looks like now, thanks to your tip."

Darla swiped a tear from her cheek. "Good. He was a nice man. He deserved better than he got."

"If there's anything you can tell us, it could stop something like that from happening again," Dean said.

Nicole watched his gaze slide meaningfully to her

and Blakely. The unspoken message loud and clear. Maybe, if they were lucky, Cari wouldn't turn up dead and pumped full of drugs like the doctor. Classified as another former user who backslid. Not worth the investigation.

Darla checked over both shoulders. "Okay. Here's how it is. The ladies are just eye candy," she said, shifting foot to foot as if she wanted to run. "We dress up and serve partygoers drinks and hors d'oeuvres from trays. We're paid to mingle and be nice. The guests are mostly rich men. We're allowed to stop work and be alone with guests anytime we want, but we don't have to. The hosts spend all night trying to get guests to invest cash in the company and buy high-end cars. If that doesn't work, they blackmail them with images taken during the night, usually of the men with servers who don't look like servers. We're told that this is all acceptable because the money is used to keep the business going, which means more jobs for us. If the men like the servers, they sometimes offer them nice white-collar jobs at their offices, or make them personal assistant at their massive homes."

She swallowed, looking a little ill. "That's all I know. Except that once in a while, if one of the guests complains about a server, she never comes back. I assumed in the past that meant she was fired. Now I don't know."

"Thank you," Nicole said. She looked to Dean to be sure they had enough information.

He nodded. "I meant what I said about the ranch.

I can call ahead and let them know you're coming. They're good people."

"No one's good people," she said, then she turned and jogged away, bypassing the shop and slipping into the shadowy space between stores, heading for the main parking lot out front.

Nicole watched her go. "Should we follow her home for her safety?"

Dean considered. "Maybe. I don't think she'd notice my tail, but if she's right about being watched, that person likely would notice. I don't want to make things worse instead of better."

Nicole's heart leaped as another thought crashed into her mind. "We should've asked where the party was tonight." She grabbed Dean's hand and started for the alley.

Darla was on the sidewalk out front when they entered the walkway between buildings.

The rumble of an engine rose on the air as Darla stepped onto the little parking lot road outside her store.

Nicole fell still as a squeal of tires and streak of blackness collided with Darla, throwing her small body up and over the hood. She crashed, lifeless, onto the tire marks left behind by the sleek black sedan.

Chapter Seventeen

Dean scrubbed a hand over his hair, stunned and gut-wrenched by the horrific scene before him.

A young woman was dead, and he hadn't been able to save her. He'd raced to her and performed chest compressions until the first responders arrived, but he'd known it was a work in futility. He'd just kept hoping he was wrong.

Nicole sat several yards away now, in Dean's truck, beneath the shade of a tree. Tears tracked down her cheeks as she entertained Blakely with a stuffed pony.

Half the available Marshal's Bluff police force was visible in the space around the tire tracks and collision site. Thankfully, the coroner had been efficient at the scene and quickly removed Darla's body from public view. A report would be available soon, but Dean didn't need anyone to tell him what had killed her. He'd never forget those details. What he wanted to know was who.

Members of the strip mall's security team assisted officers in interviewing bystanders. A few had glimpsed the event from start to finish, but many more had seen or heard the car as it raced away. Security footage from the stores was already under review.

Finn moseyed in Dean's direction, surveying the area as he made his way to the sidewalk. "Well, this has been a long and increasingly awful day."

Dean dropped his hands to his sides, then braced them on his hips, aching to be useful in some way that would end the reign of terror in his town. "Any luck identifying the car or driver?"

"Maybe. Security footage confirmed the make and model match the sedan that tailed you. There's front-end damage now, so the owner will be looking to get that repaired. We've already contacted all the local body shops and provided a heads-up. If a car fitting that description comes in for work, they're to accept and keep it, then notify the police. We've also got the dealership's garage under surveillance, since so many threads are already leading back there."

Dean grimaced, unsure how useful the surveillance team really was. Officers had been watching Mikey's home and work, but that hadn't stopped him from being beaten nearly to death outside the pizzeria. All it took was a few minutes of distraction, accidental sleep or a changing shift for something to go irrevocably wrong. "How's Mikey doing?" he asked, fearing whoever had hospitalized him and killed Darla might want to finish the job.

"He's stable now," Finn said. "Swelling's coming down in his brain and on his face. The internal bleeding was stopped, and the rest of his injuries are cast and bandaged. He's got a few broken fingers and ribs.

Fractures on both hands and his clavicle. He put up one hell of a fight from the looks of it. Austin's with him and keeping me updated after each set of rounds."

Knowing Austin was with Mikey went a long way toward easing Dean's concerns. "Have you learned anything more about Rising Tides?"

Finn blew out a long, weary breath, looking a decade older than his years. "I think the whole thing was a front. My best guess is the investment money goes straight to some offshore account. There's no evidence of any company by that name in North Carolina, and the handful of similarly named businesses in other states are either defunct or have legitimate storefronts with specific purposes. One in California is a surf shop. Another in Maine sells boating and fishing equipment. In this town, on the other hand, it seems the name was just made up for the sake of hiring clueless workers and duping investors." He squinted against the sun, frowning deeply at the growing crowd of curious onlookers. "The Dr. Maline robbery case is being reopened as a murder investigation."

Dean's brows twitched, surprise and approval swirled in his mind. "That's good." And fast. Things involving the legal system didn't typically happen this quickly, but given the circumstances, he was glad to hear the powers that be were cooperating.

"A brief look into Dr. Maline's financials revealed monthly cash withdrawals for the past seventeen months. He'd all but eviscerated his funds about a month before his death. Assuming those withdraw-

als were blackmail payoffs, whoever had been the re-
cipient likely burned him when the well ran dry. No
reason to leave a man with nothing to lose alive. He
might've finally gone to the police."

Dean grunted, hating that Cari had gotten involved
with this group, whoever they were. His fear for her
life grew exponentially with each passing second.

The gruesome thoughts were likely on Nicole's
mind as well. His attention returned to her and
Blakely. He couldn't help Cari yet, but he could take
care of her daughter and sister. "I'm going to drive
the ladies home," he told Finn. "It's hot, and this has
been a terrible day."

"Stay in touch," Finn said. He offered his fist, and
the two exchanged a short series of taps that had become a private handshake when they were younger.
The gesture was surprisingly comforting now. A reminder that the Beaumonts got through everything
that came at them. And they got through it together.

NICOLE CURLED ONTO the sofa at Dean's place that
night, legs pulled up to her chest, chin resting on her
knees. She'd soaked in his tub after Blakely went to
sleep; fatigue and steaming water had slowly cleared
her mind and relaxed her tense muscles. She'd never
forget the things she'd seen that afternoon, but a long
bath and the cool night air were working wonders to
keep her mind still and calm. For that she was im-
measurably thankful.

Dean had opened the windows, thinking the night
air would help her sleep, and she couldn't disagree.

Something about the gentle breeze drifting through the curtains was incredibly soothing to her nerves. And she suspected Dean missed being outside.

Cari's disappearance had kept him on the job non-stop for days, when he'd normally have gone fishing or hiking or spent time on the family ranch. He was an outdoorsman and a cowboy by nature and nurture, not someone who could be cooped up long without going stir-crazy.

He'd been living outside his comfort zone for Nicole without a single complaint.

"Thirsty?" He appeared barefoot before her in pale gray sweatpants and a white cotton T-shirt, a glass of cold water in each hand. His brown hair was dark and wet from the shower. Familiar scents of his soap and shampoo sent a tingle down her spine.

It was beyond unfair that the sight of him still did that to her. She missed him in ways she couldn't begin to describe.

"How's your side feel?" he asked, scanning her as he passed her a drink. "Can I get you anything for the pain?"

She set her glass on the coffee table, then she lifted the side of her shirt to reveal her fresh bandage. "It's healing. No signs of redness, swelling or infection, and I hurt less today than yesterday. I took more painkillers while you were in the shower."

"May I?" he asked, lifting a hand toward her raised shirt.

"Yeah."

He drifted careful fingers along the exposed skin

of her side, brow furrowed, expression tight. "I hate that this happened to you."

"I know." She shivered at the sensation of his touch, wishing he'd come closer, take her into his arms and make her forget about the ugliness of their day.

His Adam's apple bobbed, and his eyes flashed with heat, as if he'd somehow read her mind. He pulled his hand away and straightened, allowing her shirt to fall back into place. "Did I hear the phone ring while I was in the shower?"

She nodded, embarrassed by her need. Thankful he couldn't read her mind. "Yeah. Our moms called. Mom made it to the ranch and had a late dinner with your folks. She wanted to see Blakely tonight, but she'd already fallen asleep, so I told Mom about our day and promised we'd come for breakfast in the morning."

"Sounds like a plan. I'm glad she made it."

"Me, too." Nicole's stomach clenched at the thought of seeing her mother. She missed her terribly, and felt guilty for putting her off, but it'd been a long week. Nicole had to be the strong one whenever her mother was upset, but she couldn't do that tonight.

"I was thinking," Dean said, his voice soft and casual. "It might be best to leave Blakely at the ranch tomorrow instead of taking her with us again. Truthfully, I think you should consider staying there, too. It's the safest place for you both, and having you there will be an incredible comfort to your mother."

Nicole turned on the cushion, dropping her knees and facing him. "What if I want to stay with you?"

she asked. The unintentionally deeper meaning lowered her voice.

Surprise flickered over Dean's expression, widening his eyes and lifting his brows for an instant before he hid it away.

She wanted to stay with Dean long after Cari was found and this nightmare ended. She wanted to make up for leaving him when she should've been there for him, and she wanted to make up for lost time. Because since the moment she'd first met Dean Beaumont, her heart and soul had belonged to him and him alone.

"If you stay with me, I'll protect you and care for you as long as you want to be here," he said.

Her heart thundered and her breath caught.

A look of torture tightened his jaw. "We should probably talk about some things when this is over and Cari is home," he said slowly. "Emotions are high right now, and you're going through more than anyone ever should. I don't want to add to that. And I don't want to make assumptions. I just want to be here for you."

Nicole inched closer, struggling to find her voice. She wanted him to make assumptions. To make a move. To read her mind.

She wanted him to want her. "You don't mind me being here?"

"No." Dean's voice was low as he lifted her hand in his and pressed her palm against his chest. "You've always been right here."

A small gasp parted her lips as his eyes searched hers.

Slowly, he erased the remaining distance between

them, cupping her face in his hands and guiding her mouth to his. The press of their lips and tangling of their breaths sent a rush of bliss from her core.

Memories of a thousand shared moments like this one whirled in her heart and head. Dean was her safe place. Her emotional haven and physical comfort. He was her perfect match in every way, and she wanted him back, body and soul.

"Dean," she whispered, head falling back as he dragged his mouth down the column of her throat. "Touch me."

He wrapped big hands around her hips and lifted her onto his lap, her thighs bracketing his. Rough palms slid beneath the hem of her shirt, long fingers curving over her ribs. The pads of his thumbs brushed the sensitive undersides of her bare breasts, and she was never so thankful to have skipped a bra with her pajamas.

Dean's deep moan of pleasure quickly became a growl as the material shifted higher, exposing her fully. His hungry gaze climbed to meet hers, and she smiled.

A curse slid from his mouth as he splayed one hand across her back and lowered his lips to one taut nipple. He teased and lavished her with nips and sucks until a deep ache formed between her thighs.

The cool night breeze arched her back and pulled her skin into a cascade of goose bumps. A delicious contrast to the heat of his hands and mouth. And Nicole wanted more.

She tugged restlessly at his shirt, desperate to remove the barriers between them.

He released her, reluctantly, and freed them both of their shirts in seconds.

Then he dragged the pad of one thumb across her kiss-swollen lips, then studied her bare, flushed breasts with reverence. Indecision warred on his brow.

"Dean," she whispered, gripping his chin and locking him in her stare. She slowly rocked her hips against the hard length of him. "Take me to bed."

His hands were on her backside in a heartbeat, gripping her to him and rising in one fluid movement, taking her with him as he stood. "Are you sure this is what you want?" he asked, voice husky with desire, eyes patient and kind.

"I want you," she answered. "Only you. Always you."

His mouth twisted into the smug, satisfied grin she loved, and his mouth met hers once more as he carried her to his room.

Chapter Eighteen

Nicole woke the next morning wrapped in Dean's arms. His long, lean body was pressed to hers. Their legs tangled beneath a single sheet. Fresh summer air drifted through his bedroom curtains.

"Morning," he said, trailing kisses over her forehead and temple, cheek and jaw. His arms tightened gently, gathering her closer.

She twined their fingers and nuzzled against him. "I don't want to leave this bed or this room," she said. "Or this moment."

He rolled her onto her back and hovered over her, dotting her nose and each corner of her mouth with more light kisses.

She squeezed her eyes shut, pushing away thoughts of a new day and the troubles awaiting them outside the blissful bubble.

Dean gathered her wrists in his hands and stretched her arms above her head. His eyes skimmed her body, and he lowered his mouth to her shoulder.

Maybe she could ignore the day a little while longer.

His phone rang, and he lifted his face to frown in the device's direction.

She smiled while he seemed to consider whether or not to answer.

Eventually, he sat back on his heels, taking the sheet with him. His eyes skimmed her fully exposed body. "Life is truly unfair."

"Truly," she agreed.

The phone rang again, and he reached for it with a sigh. "It's Mama."

Blakely fussed a moment later, and Nicole grabbed one of Dean's shirts on the way to soothe her, dressing as she went.

No more life in a bubble.

Blakely was awake in her portable crib, kicking her feet and cooing at dust motes on sunbeams when Nicole arrived.

"Hello, sweet baby girl," Nicole said, pulling her niece into her arms. "I bet you're ready to get changed and have a little breakfast. What do you say?"

She combed Blakely's hair into its usual tiny ponytail on top and selected a flowing A-line tank top with spaghetti straps and layers of lavender ruffles that emphasized her round little belly. Paired with matching stretchy bike shorts, she was the definition of adorable.

Nicole was sure Dean's mama was calling about breakfast. Her mother was likely eager to see her granddaughter, and Nicole couldn't make her wait a second longer than necessary. She also agreed with his declaration from the previous night. Blakely would be safer on the ranch than staying with Dean and Nicole. Too many people were getting hurt now. She couldn't allow her niece to become one of them.

Nicole raked a brush through her thick waves and pulled them into a ponytail. She dressed in jean shorts and a faded Marshal's Bluff Athletics T-shirt. The outfit was cute and comfortable, which was perfect, because assuming the last few days were anything to go by, there was another long day ahead. But at least, whatever came, she would be with Dean.

"Nicole." Her name rose on his voice through the air, and the fine hair on her neck and arms stood at attention. She gathered Blakely to her and hurried in the direction of the sound.

"Yeah?"

His expression was hard, and he held his cell phone on one palm. "I've got Finn on speaker. She's here," he said, glancing at the device. "Go on."

Nicole's muscles tightened and her stomach coiled. Was this the moment she learned Cari had been found, and she wasn't okay? Were they too late, like Dean had been while searching for eight-year-old Ben Smothers?

"Morning, Nicole," Finn said. "I'm just providing an update. No real news just yet."

Her shoulders drooped, and she heaved a ragged sigh. "Okay," she croaked. "Thank you."

"I secured a warrant to search all records at the auto dealership," he said. "That hit-and-run motivated the judge, so I'm taking some officers with me to get started right away. Also, one of the men working in the garage lied about where he was on the night of the party, which garnered my interest. A background check came back dirty. Criminal past, gang affiliations in Charlotte, and no friends I could find among his coworkers. He worked exclusively on all Tippin's cars, and Tippin's clients' cars. The clients asked for him by name when they needed service, which wasn't company policy, more like grace offered to the dealership's biggest seller. Now that we've established a relationship between the two men, we're looking for the mechanic. His name is Joseph Knolls. We think he might also be the driver of the black sedan that hit Darla and chased you guys."

Nicole watched Dean's face for clues on how to interpret Finn's news, but Dean's expression was flat. "What does this mean?" she asked. Bigger questions mounted with each new heartbeat. Would they find Cari when they found Knolls? Did they know where to look? What exactly had the man's criminal past involved? Was he violent? Did he hurt women?

"It means I think this is the lead we needed to break the case. I think Knolls knows where the Tippins are hiding and what happened to your sister."

Dean pulled the phone closer to his mouth. "We're headed to the ranch to see Nicole's mom. She made it into town last night. Where will you be in an hour or so?" His gaze lifted to meet Nicole's.

"Likely at the dealership. Give me a call when you leave the ranch. And Nicole?"

She looked to the phone. "Yeah?"

"We're getting close."

THE BEAUMONT RANCH was a few miles outside town, located on more than one hundred acres of land passed down through the family for generations. From what Nicole had been told, the place was even larger once, but fringe acreage had been sold off in parcels over the years, especially during hard times, to keep the ranch up and running. Other portions had long ago been given to extended family members as wedding gifts, but those plots had been sold and resold to owners who likely had no idea the family who'd originally owned them was still thriving next door.

Dean turned onto the long gravel lane that led to the ranch. His family's name was branded into a massive slab of wood fastened to the wrought iron gate. Nicole's lips curved into a smile as they bounced along the gently pitted path toward Dean's childhood home.

Their mothers rose from rocking chairs on the wide wraparound porch, heading for the steps before the truck was parked. Both women wore jeans and tennis shoes with untucked T-shirts and tired smiles.

Dean stopped the truck in a wide space meant for turnarounds, and Nicole climbed out, suddenly desperate to get her arms around her mother. She hoped she wouldn't be disappointed that Nicole had let something bad happen to her sister.

"Honey!" Nicole's mom pulled her into a tight embrace, tears streaming. "I'm so sorry you've been going through this alone," she said, stepping back to look into her eyes. "I should've been here."

"I wasn't alone," Nicole said, hoping to put her

mom's concern at ease. "I've been with Dean, and his brothers are helping every day. You came as soon as you could. How are Grandma and Grandpa?"

"Fine." Her mom sniffled, shame and guilt clouding her face. She was otherwise beautiful and lithe with the same dark curls, brown eyes and dusting of freckles as her daughters and granddaughter. In many ways it was like looking into a mirror for Nicole, except there were creases on her mother's face that hadn't yet appeared on her own.

"I love you," her mother whispered, snapping Nicole's gaze back to hers. "I don't say that enough. Spending all this time with my parents has made me realize a few things. One of those is how much I love you girls. Another is how much I relied on you when things were tough with Cari, then the divorce, and that was wrong of me." She slid her soft palms to Nicole's cheeks. "I'm sorry for every moment you felt abandoned by me, or as if you needed to be strong for me. That was never your role to play."

Tears blurred Nicole's eyes, sliding hot and fast over her cheeks as she hugged her mom again. She hadn't known how much she'd needed to hear those words until they were presented. "I love you, too."

Blakely squealed with glee, and the sound broke them apart.

Nicole's mother laughed nervously, then kissed her cheek and turned to Mrs. Beaumont, who'd collected Blakely from her car seat.

"Lucky grandma," Mrs. Beaumont said. "You only have two girls, and you already got a grandbaby. I've got five boys," she said, tossing a mischievous look in Dean's direction. "And not a single one of these." She nuzzled her nose against Blakely's neck, causing a sharp squeal of delight. "It doesn't seem fair."

Nicole's mom pulled Blakely into her arms with gentle care, as if she were the most precious thing on earth.

A tangible connection to her own missing child.

Mrs. Beaumont clapped her hands. "Hope y'all are hungry. We've been cooking all morning." She looped one arm through Dean's and the other through Nicole's. "Let's go. There's plenty for everyone."

Nicole's mom followed, snuggling Blakely tight.

Dean stayed at Nicole's side throughout the meal, a hand on her back, fingers grazing her hip or curled over her knee beneath the table.

As if the connection they'd made last night had meant as much to him as it had to her. And just for the moment, she let herself hope.

Chapter Nineteen

Dean took Nicole's hand as they left Blakely and their moms on the porch after breakfast. He didn't miss his mama's prideful, cat-that-ate-the-canary grin as she watched him reach for Nicole. And he hadn't been able to quash his echoing smile as Nicole accepted his touch, folding their fingers easily together.

Nicole's reunion with her mother had been hard on her; it was written on her face beneath the smile. In the set of her jaw and pinch of her lips. She'd likely internalized Cari's situation as her fault somehow, though she logically knew better. That was any decent sibling's cross to bear. An unspoken, deeply rooted acceptance of responsibility. Dean had been glad to hear her mom tell her this situation wasn't her fault, but the words hadn't stuck. Nicole had been the strong one in their family for too long, and it would take time to ease that burden.

He could also see that walking away from her hurting mother right now was hard. Her every instinct probably told her to stay and provide comfort. And leaving Blakely was one more heart-wrenching choice. Cari had asked Nicole to care for her baby. But the weight of the week had taken its toll, and Dean knew she needed space and time more than she needed to continue giving bits of herself to others. So he ushered her along, hoping she wouldn't change her mind.

Everyone needed a break and a safe place to recuperate.

He wanted to be that place for her.

She was silent as they buckled up inside the truck and pulled away from the ranch.

Soon Dean navigated the desolate country roads on autopilot. His mind was back in the homey farmhouse kitchen his mama adored. Sharing a meal with Nicole and her mom had been a more emotional experience than he'd anticipated. They'd shared dozens of meals like that one in the past, often with his father and brothers as well, but everything had been different this time. Not just the specific circumstances, but the fact that their time together was limited. If he didn't convince her to give him another chance, he could lose her for good. The possibility twisted his gut.

Beside him, Nicole unearthed her phone and tapped the screen. A minute later, Cari's voice arrived through the speaker. Nicole replayed the video her sister had sent for Blakely on the night she'd disappeared.

"They're all wearing black dresses," Nicole whispered. "Just like Darla said." She turned to face him, and her gaze heated his cheek. "If that guy would run her down in cold blood like that, in the middle of the

day, outside a store, what's he been doing to my sister all this time?" Her voice cracked, and he reached
for her again.

"Hey," he said, covering her free hand with his.
"We're going to find her."

"How do you know?"

He didn't, and statistically, things didn't look good,
but Cari was tough and resilient. Those qualities would
serve her well. And he wasn't willing to break Nicole's
heart as long as there was still room for hope. "You
heard Finn this morning," he said instead. "He's close.
So we're going to hang in there just a little while longer
before we start letting panic sound the alarm bells."

She nodded and broke their connection to wipe
beneath her eyes.

Dean pressed the button on his steering wheel to
make a phone call, shaking off the nonsensical sting
of rejection. "Call Finn."

"Calling Finn," the automated female voice responded.

Nicole played Cari's video again, her sister's happy
voice sounding against the background of fellow waitstaff chatter and the echo of closing car doors. "She's
got the frame so tight on her face, I can't tell where
she was," Nicole complained. "We saw a shuttle drop
her off at the Tippins' place. This is somewhere else.
Where?"

"Hello, brother," Finn said, his words arriving
through the truck's speakers. "How was breakfast?"

Nicole looked to the dashboard. "Hi, Finn," she
answered.

"Breakfast was good," Dean added. "Any news?"

"Hey, Nicole. Nothing solid yet, but my gut says something's about to give."

Dean grunted, feeling much the same, but unsure why, specifically.

"What are you guys up to?" Finn asked.

"We're just leaving the ranch," Dean said. "Where are you?"

"Headed back to the dealership. I just left tech services. They're deep into Cari's phone. She didn't have tracking engaged, so they're concentrating on her contacts, recent communication and social media connections."

"Nicole's watching that good-night video Cari sent Blakely," Dean said.

As if on cue, Nicole's fingers curled over his arm.

A single glance in her direction told him something had happened. Her eyes were wide, her lips parted. She'd paused the video and held the phone near her ear. "You okay?" he asked, unsure what he'd missed.

"I think I hear an alarm," she said.

Dean frowned.

"What?" Finn asked.

Nicole held her phone closer to Dean's and played the video again. "Ignore Cari and listen to the other girls' laughter."

Dean's foot eased off the gas, attention hyper-focused on the background noises.

It was barely there, but it was something. A buzzer?

"What is it?" Finn asked. "Play it again."

Nicole moved her phone toward the dashboard and played it again.

"That's the drawbridge alarm," Finn said. "Change of plans. Meet me down there. I'll call Kim in tech and tell her to isolate the sound in case we're wrong, then I'll ask if they've found anything else on the phone to suggest Cari spent time in that area during the days or weeks before her disappearance."

"There are a lot of warehouses near the water," Dean said. "Would be a good place for the servers to meet up and catch the shuttle."

"Agreed," Finn said. "Nice work, Nicole. See y'all in a few."

The call disconnected, and Nicole flopped back in her seat, hugging her phone to her chest.

They zipped along the outskirts of town toward the bay, taking back roads to avoid stoplights and traffic. The silence between them was charged with anticipation, and their fingers were twined on the seat between them. Whatever happened, they were in this together, and he'd be here for her however he could. For as long as she'd allow him.

The pretty rural scenery quickly morphed into the battered gray of the waterfront, where fields and farmland were swapped for business parks and concrete. Clouds blocked the morning sunshine, reflecting their dreariness onto the water.

They slowed when the drawbridge came into view, and an unpleasant sense of foreboding slithered into his core.

Beside him, Nicole played the video again.

They drove through every parking lot and alley within earshot of the drawbridge alarm, searching for Cari's missing car, or a reasonable place to stash it. Someplace the servers would meet up and wait for their ride. Maybe even a sign with the words *Rising Tides*.

The truck crawled past a row of triple-stacked shipping containers along the waterfront, waiting to be moved or packed. A motionless barge floated just offshore.

"Look," Nicole whispered, turning the phone to Dean. She'd paused the video again and zoomed in on the space above Cari's shoulder. The edge of a rust-colored building or possibly a shipping container. The tip of a blue streak visible. Maybe the work of a street artist or more of the area's abundant graffiti.

The containers beside them showed no signs of spray paint.

"What is it?" he asked, unsure what to make of the unidentified corner.

"Train car?"

It only took a moment for Dean to process the words and perform a smooth three-point turn in the narrow alley. Then they were headed north, away from the drawbridge by another block, moving swiftly toward the tracks.

His phone rang, and Finn's name appeared on the dashboard screen.

Dean pressed the button to answer.

"I've got something," Finn said, foregoing a greeting. "A picture sent to Cari from several weeks ago had a geotag. Looks like it was taken at a warehouse near the train tracks."

Dean exchanged a look with Nicole, who'd gone still at his side. "We're on it," Dean said. "Meet us there?"

"Already on my way."

The call disconnected as a pint-sized metal building with several parking spaces and roll-up garage doors came into view. The structure was across from the tracks and positioned in the shadows of multiple larger buildings.

The black entry door had two words painted on the security window.

Rising Tides.

NICOLE SHOOK AS she jumped down from Dean's cab, unsure what to say to whoever was inside the building. Would the people here run away like Mikey had? Would they lie like the Tippins? Or try to hurt her and Dean the way the driver of the black sedan had hurt Darla?

Dean met her at the truck's hood and reached for her hand.

Something in the unseasonably cool air and mass of ominous clouds set her intuition on high alert, making her doubly glad Blakely wasn't with them now.

They paused before the door, and Dean tried the knob. When the knob didn't turn, he rang the buzzer.

No one answered, so he knocked.

Then he pounded.

"Hello?" he called.

Nicole jumped at the sudden, deep and authoritative boom of his voice.

He grinned down at her, then released her hand. "Stay right here."

He jogged the few feet to his truck and came back with his lock-picking tools. "Finn's on the way, so I have to hurry."

Nicole watched as he selected two pieces from the small leather pouch, then got to work.

A moment later, Dean turned the knob, and the door opened.

He raised an arm in front of her before she could step inside. He tipped his finger to his lips, warning her to be quiet. "Hello?" he called, projecting his voice inside.

The deep tenor echoed through the cavernous interior, and a soft shuffling sound returned on the breeze.

Nicole raised her brows. Was someone hiding inside? Was Cari tied up and held captive?

Dean stepped forward, tucking Nicole behind him. "Marshal's Bluff Police," he called.

Nicole gave his arm a reproachful shove. Impersonating an officer was a major offense.

He shrugged, then took her hand and moved inside, leaving the door open behind them.

Several silent steps later, the short, narrow walkway opened into a vast, dimly lit space. The shuttle from the video came into view several yards away. The same ride that had delivered Cari to the Tippins' home.

Beside it stood Cari's car.

The sound of an approaching vehicle outside the open door sent Dean against the wall, pulling her with him. Together, they waited, motionless and watching the lot outside.

A moment later, Finn's cruiser pulled into the spot beside Dean's truck.

He climbed out with a frown, then marched inside, head shaking at the sight of them. "What are you two doing in here?"

"Door was open," Dean said, straight-faced and voice level.

Nicole averted her gaze.

"Uh-huh." Finn glanced back at the door's knob and dead bolt, frown deepening. "What'd you find?"

"This is as far as we got," Dean said, "but there's a lot to see so far."

Finn followed them to the end of the hall, and his gaze jumped to the vehicles on the warehouse floor. "Cari's car?"

Nicole nodded, still shocked by the vehicle's presence. She hoped it was a sign they'd soon find Cari as well.

She moved with the Beaumonts as they closed in on the parked shuttle and car.

A small office with a large window looked over the wide-open floor. A desk, computer and filing cabinets were visible through the glass.

Finn called dispatch as they walked, reporting the findings and requesting his team's immediate presence.

Nicole's heart thrummed with anticipation, and Dean's grip on her hand tightened in response. Someone had busted the driver's-side window, scattering fragments of glass over the warehouse floor.

Dean dug his phone from one pocket and accessed the device's flashlight app. He shone the beam into the car.

There weren't any signs of Cari or her things inside. Only Blakely's empty car seat.

Finn tucked his phone away. "The team's en route. Try not to touch anything." He pulled a set of blue gloves from his pocket and passed one to Dean. "We're going to have to share." They each pulled a glove over their right hand.

"I can look through Cari's car," Nicole suggested. "No glove necessary. My prints are probably on everything in there already."

"It's still a crime scene," Finn said. "You can look, but try not to touch. Use your phone's light. Take pictures, make mental notes. Talk to the team when they get here about anything that strikes you as odd or wrong."

Finn turned toward the office thirty feet away. "I'm starting in there."

Dean hovered, staring into the thick line of shadows against a nearby wall, then scanning the warehouse from top to bottom, paying careful attention to the catwalk overhead and a door on the rear wall. "When the team arrives, they'll break up and check every inch of this place. I'd say this is ground zero."

Nicole trembled.

Dean gave the larger scene another cursory look. "It's a clean warehouse. Probably just used to store the transport vehicle and possibly the waitstaff's cars while they're at a gig. It shouldn't be too hard to find out who owns or leases the space. And any evidence uncovered here won't have been exposed to the elements or a lot of people, which means the findings will be less contaminated."

His phone rang, and he turned it over in his hand while Nicole peered into the car. "Hey, Austin," he said. "Get down to the tracks by the drawbridge."

Nicole's spirits lifted by a measure. The Beaumonts were circling the wagons. They were closer to finding Cari than they'd ever been, or at least finding the person responsible for her absence. Finn and Dean were on-site already, with Austin and members of the Marshal's Bluff PD on the way.

Lights flipped on inside the small office across the large space, where Finn opened filing cabinet drawers and riffled through the contents.

Dean moved back toward the small hallway and open warehouse door. "No," he said. "We're on the north end."

Nicole circled to the other side of the car, keeping both Beaumonts in her sights, then she opened the passenger door, not wanting to disturb the broken glass.

She illuminated her phone's light and squatted outside the open door, peering under the passenger seat for clues.

The distant creak of metal turned her head as a heavy hand clamped over her mouth. The oddly familiar scent, which she now recognized as motor oil, lodged in her nose, and a knife pressed against her throat.

"If you want to see your sister alive, you're coming with me," he whispered, already pulling her away from Cari's car and into the shadows.

Chapter Twenty

Dean gave Austin directions to the little warehouse tucked among the much larger ones, keeping one eye on Nicole in case she needed him. Seeing her sister's car had likely upset her more than she let on, but he didn't want to press. There was much work to be done.

She rounded the silver compact to the far side and opened the passenger door, crouching low. The light from her phone flashed on. Maybe she was truly inspecting the vehicle, but Dean suspected it was her way of gaining a little space as well.

Austin arrived a moment later, taking his time to climb down from his truck and meet Dean at the open warehouse door.

Cari's car door was still open, Nicole still out of sight as he led Austin to the small office on the opposite side of the warehouse.

Dean itched to go to her when she didn't pop up to greet Austin. He stared at the car, willing her to call to him, not wanting to intrude.

"Y'all are going to want to take a look at this," Finn said.

Dean and Austin pushed through the office door in single file.

Finn was on the phone with a smug grin. "Send a tow truck," he said, one finger pointed to a set of computer screens on the corner of the desk.

A black-and-white image of the Charger that had hit and killed Darla sat in a parking lot monitored by the camera. The same car that had chased him, Nicole and Blakely.

The satisfied look on his brother's face spread to Dean as well. He poked his head through the doorway to the area beyond. This was a good enough reason to interrupt Nicole.

He projected his voice into the cavernous space. "Nicole!"

"I wonder why he didn't he park the car inside?" Austin asked. "If he brought it here to hide it, why leave it in the lot?"

Dean stared into the warehouse that suddenly felt much larger and more ominous than before. The absence of movement and absolute lack of response from Nicole echoed all around them. Then he dragged his attention back to the security monitor.

Joseph Knolls hadn't pulled his car inside yet, because they'd arrived and interrupted him.

Nicole appeared on the small screen, being dragged across the lot at knifepoint.

NICOLE'S CHEST ACHED with every ragged breath, the knife scraping at her throat as they moved through the rear lot. She longed to scream, to fight, to let him cut her throat right there and take her chances at survival when emergency responders arrived.

But her abductor had mentioned Cari.

He knew where she was, and though she might already be dead, and he could be a liar, there wasn't any choice to make. If there was a chance that leaving with him meant seeing Cari again, she had to go. Because maybe she could help her.

She squinted against the assaulting outdoor light and struggled to keep pace with her attacker.

Trickles of wet heat rolled over the column of her throat. Sweat or blood, she wasn't sure. The knife was sharp, and their jagged, uncoordinated movements could easily send the blade into her skin. It'd happened before.

He lowered the knife to adjust his hold on her, and she nearly doubled over in relief. "Drop the cell phone. Now."

He pressed the button on a key fob, unlocking the doors of his car, and yanked the phone from her stiff wooden fingers when she didn't comply. Then he shoved her toward a familiar black sedan.

Her stomach pitted and lurched.

It was the car she'd seen kill Darla, the front light still broken from where her body had collided with the plastic. Images of the hit-and-run sent splinters of ice through Nicole's veins as he opened the driver's side-door and shoved her inside.

"Move," he barked. "Get into the passenger seat." He locked the doors and took up position behind the wheel.

The car peeled backward before she could get seated, and in her side-view mirror, three outraged Beaumonts raced into the lot too late, guns drawn.

The man beside her snickered. He wore baggy jeans and brown work boots, mostly unlaced and dark with oil. A gray T-shirt underscored his scowl. He appeared to be in his late thirties, with a scar running across his forehead and through one eyebrow. Heavy acne scars marred his cheeks.

She would never forget his face, and she committed every detail to memory in case she lived to describe it.

The needle on the dashboard climbed with their increasing speed, and she worked to fasten her seat belt before he jammed the brakes and threw her into the windshield.

He tore around corners, taking a nonsensical path away from the warehouse and waterfront. Making it harder for anyone to follow.

Then they were on the highway, flying over the bridge and looking down on the section of town where they'd just been.

A line of police cruisers stormed the area below, lights blazing.

But she was already gone.

"Are you taking me to my sister?" Nicole asked, forcing the words up a shrinking windpipe. Fear, trauma and distress lightened her head and tilted the car beneath her.

He didn't respond.

She tested her seat belt, unsure what he might do

to her while driving and not wanting to find out. She rested her palm over the button to unlatch her restraint, guarding it as she spoke again. "Are you taking me to Cari? Are you the one who took her from the Tippins' house?"

His jaw tensed, the only indication that he'd heard her. A suggestion she'd hit a nerve.

"Please tell me about my sister," she asked, carefully. "Is she okay? Where did you take her? Is that where we're going?"

"Shut. Up." His teeth snapped over each word, lips curled back in a snarl.

Nicole bit her tongue, stomach clenched and toes curled in terror. She watched the passing exit signs and the clock, calculating the amount of miles and minutes that passed.

Too much and too many.

Memories of Darla's confession rushed into her mind, along with the Tippins' absence. If the car salesman was the leader of this crime ring, was his mechanic just the muscle? Was it possible the man beside her was also a victim somehow? Maybe being blackmailed, too? It seemed possible that Knolls could be a pawn in Tippin's awful game.

She could only imagine what kind of information Tippin must have on someone to make them do the things Knolls had done.

"Does Mr. Tippin make you do this so his hands stay clean?" she asked. The words were out of her mouth before she thought better of them. "Does he force you to do his grunt work while he and his wife run off and hide?" Days' worth of anger, frustration and fear attached themselves to each syllable, making her tone unintentionally snide and condescending.

"What did you say?" His face jerked in her direction as he raced along the highway, yanking the steering wheel left, then right with barely a glance. The Charger flew in and out of lanes, barely missing a hatchback and cutting off a semitruck.

Nicole's hands curled around her safety belt. She straightened in her seat, prepared for the inevitable crash and hoping she'd survive it. Though surviving seemed unlikely at 120 miles per hour with nothing but pavement, large moving vehicles and a concrete divide to stop them.

"I'm no one's errand boy," he seethed. "We're partners. He couldn't do his job without me. I'm the one who makes everything possible."

"By everything you mean the blackmail, abduction and murder?" Nicole asked, all sense of self-preservation having gone completely out the window. Anger welled in her. If death was imminent, she at least wanted one answer. "Where is my sister?" she screamed.

He cut through multiple lanes, cruising at top speed to an off-ramp and earning a series of outraged honks from drivers behind them.

"I should've asked where Mr. Tippin told you to take her," she said, tired of being the victim and desperate to hurt him in some small way for all the pain he'd already caused her. "You don't need to lie to me. The police have already seen the files. Talked to everyone at the dealership, too. Darla and Mikey told us you're nothing more than a henchman and an underling, Joseph Knolls." She spoke his name with emphasis. If he'd been surprised she knew Tippin's name, she suspected he'd be doubly shocked to know his gig was up, too.

A grease-stained hand flew out to connect with her temple, and her head slammed into the passenger window before her world went black.

Chapter Twenty-One

Nicole's eyes opened to a thunderous sound. Sharp pain spiked in her head and neck. Her ears rang and stomach coiled. Then the ground fell out from beneath her.

"Wake up," an ugly but familiar voice demanded, catching her before she rolled out of the car.

Above her, light lanced her eyes. Beneath her, the hands of her attacker gripped and tugged, dragging her into the day. Before her a cavernous opening loomed.

It took several seconds for her addled brain to recognize the location as a storage facility. The noise that had awoken her was likely the sound of the heavy door being rolled upward.

Now, Joseph Knolls shoved her toward the stacks of boxes.

She struggled to make sense of the situation. He was supposed to take her to her sister. "Cari," she choked, the voice not sounding like her own. "Where's Cari?"

He pushed hard against her shoulders, thrusting

her toward the nearest wall before retreating and rolling the door down behind him.

A moment later, sounds of the car's engine grew
distant and disappeared.

Bits of light filtered in around the door, and a small,
narrow beam flashed on. The soft glow climbed her
noodle legs and trembling chest.

"Nicole!" Cari's voice cracked and warbled in the
darkness.

"Cari!"

Her sister appeared, barely more than a silhouette,
flashlight in hand. Her thin arms wrapped around Nicole, embracing and guiding her through the boxes
to a small camp near the back. A pop-up chair with
a car logo emblazoned on the material stood beside
piles of identical stadium blankets with the name of
the car dealership where Tippin and Knolls worked.

Tucked away together in the little nook, Nicole
hugged her sister long and hard, afraid to ever let go.
"I can't believe you're here. You're alive. Did he hurt
you? What happened?" She pressed a palm against
her throbbing temple and found a knot the size of an
egg. That wasn't good.

Cari directed her to the pop-up chair and helped
her sit. Even in the dim light, it was easy to see she
was filthy and gaunt, her face and arms littered with
bruising, some marks much darker than others.

The pungent smell of sweat and urine registered
belatedly, and Nicole stifled a gag.

"I'm okay," Cari said. "But you're bleeding."

Nicole touched her head again, still processing the

new circumstances. Had her sister been locked alone in a dark storage room in the southern summer heat all this time? Did she have access to water? To food? What had been Knolls's plan? To leave her for dead?

Her stomach twisted at the thought, and she pressed her lips tight.

"Your throat," Cari said softly.

Nicole shook her head, then winced from the pain. The knife had cut her, but it wasn't deep. "It'll heal."

Cari nodded, eyes filled with tears. "Nicole—" She inhaled a ragged breath, then set one hand on hers. "Where's Blakely?"

"She's safe," Nicole said quickly. There was so much to tell Cari. So much she needed to know. And so many questions Nicole had for her as well. "She's at the Beaumont Ranch with Mom."

"She's safe?" Cari asked, voice wobbling and face bright with relief. "Mom's here?"

"Yeah. Everyone's looking for you. And they're close to finding the guy who left us here, but I don't know when they'll find this place. I don't even know where we are."

"It's a storage unit owned by the car dealership where Mr. Tippin works," Cari said. "All this stuff is old. Like by a decade. I've been through most of it. I doubt anyone other than him even knows this place exists anymore. Everything in here still has the old logo I remember from commercials when I was little."

Nicole scanned the dim, sweltering space. "Tell me what happened. I've been looking for you since the morning after you went to work that catering job and didn't come home. The Beaumonts have been helping."

Cari lowered onto the piled blankets and began to sob. "I'm so sorry. I knew better than to keep taking jobs with Rising Tides, but I was trying to save money before you went back to work. I kept thinking I could turn everything around, make up for all my bad choices. And look at what happened. I'm so foolish."

"This isn't your fault," Nicole said, pushing away from the chair and joining Cari on the floor. "It's not foolish to want something more or better for you and Blakely. People like the ones running Rising Tides shouldn't exist in the world. This shouldn't have happened. You should be able to take evening jobs and not have to worry about getting involved in a blackmail ring just by being there."

"You know about that?"

"We knew everything," Nicole said. "Except how to find you."

Cari grimaced. "The money was really good. Easy. Quick. We met at a warehouse by the water, left our cars there and took a shuttle to the events. The other women told me it was so the valet wouldn't have to park so many extra cars. So the neighborhood streets wouldn't be as packed with vehicles. And so we could drink a little if we wanted and not have to drive right away. I think Tippin and Knolls just wanted an extra measure of control."

Nicole wrapped an arm around Cari's narrow shoulders and tugged her near. She wondered how many times Cari had replayed the story in her mind

since being locked in here. How many times she'd
wished for someone to tell. Someone to help her sort
out the unthinkable.

"I think some of the women slept with party guests
for extra money," Cari said, darting a glance in Nicole's
direction. "I just wanted to go to college and make
something respectable of myself. I wanted Blakely to
be proud of me. For you to be proud of me."

"You are respectable. You don't have to try. You're
good and worthy. Your past is in the past, and I am
proud of you," Nicole assured. "Always, and no matter what."

Cari wiped freshly falling tears. "We were con-
stantly offered champagne, especially on the shuttle.
I guess it was supposed to loosen us up. I never had
any. I'm probably overly cautious, but I avoid all sub-
stances. I know I had a problem before. I don't want
to go through that again. In hindsight, I think there
was something in the champagne."

"What were the parties like?"

"Sometimes servers paired off with guests and left
the party for a while. The rest of us just mingled. We
carried trays with finger foods and drinks. I made a
lot of small talk and pretended not to have any friends
or family. It seemed dangerous to tell anyone anything real. At the last party, a new guy got a little
handsy, and I noticed the shuttle driver, Knolls, was
watching. He tipped his head in the guy's direction,
as if I should accommodate him. That was the end
for me. I knew I couldn't keep working those parties.
I didn't belong there. So, I excused myself to use the

bathroom, grabbed my jacket from the kitchen and headed out the back door."

Nicole held her sister tighter, and Cari's head leaned onto her shoulder.

"I walked to a park behind their house, at the bottom of a hill to call for a ride. I sat on a bench and ordered an Uber. The app said the nearest car was nine minutes away, and I saw the twinkle lights in the trees, so I walked over there to kill some time and get out of the open, in case someone from the party noticed me. A few of the guests and servers were on the patio by the pool."

"That's when you found the bridge," Nicole said.

"I loved it. I sent you the picture because it was so perfect. Blakely would love it."

Nicole could hear her sister's smile in the words. "We found your phone there."

Cari shuddered. "I heard people talking nearby when I took the picture. The flash went off, and I startled them. Apparently the conversation was top secret, and Knolls came looking for the cause. He was so mad when he saw me. First I shut down the handsy party guest, then I left without telling anyone. He was yelling and wild-eyed before he got near me. I freaked out and ran. I dropped my phone but there wasn't time to get it. It hit the bridge then fell through the slats. When he caught me, he wanted to know what I heard. He wanted my phone. He thought I took his picture and recorded something I shouldn't. I thought he'd kill me, so I lied and told him I hid the phone. I dropped my keys in the process and didn't even notice. He was mad about that, too."

"You were smart to get out of there. You didn't belong, and you made good choices when it counted. I'm really proud of you for every one of them."

Cari tipped forward, hugging her knees to her chest and releasing her sister. "He comes here every day to try to convince me to tell him where I hid my phone."

She'd used the word *convince*, but based on the bruises covering her sister's frame, she'd really meant Knolls tried to beat the truth out of her.

And she hadn't told.

It explained why Joseph Knolls had been circling the Tippins' block. He was looking for Cari's cell phone. Trying to eliminate evidence of his crimes.

And he'd had to break into her car at the warehouse, because she'd lost her keys in the foot chase.

"He thought I was the persona I'd made up," Cari said, her tears dry and voice distant. "So he tossed me in here, said I was a junkie with no one who loved me, and if I didn't tell him what he wanted, he'd leave me to die alone and no one would even notice."

Nicole's temper flared as she kissed her sister's head. "No one has ever been more wrong. Everyone is searching for you, and when he comes back tomorrow, we're going to be ready."

Chapter Twenty-Two

Dean paced his parents' kitchen the next morning, while his brothers and father ate as if they were headed into battle and this might be their last meal. Dean couldn't even think about eating. He'd watched the man who stabbed Nicole drag her into his car and peel away. Knife to her throat this time.

The car that'd killed another young woman had been sitting outside the warehouse where he was the entire time, and he'd never even thought about walking the exterior perimeter.

Worse, a seasoned criminal and killer had been right there with them, probably watching and listening, waiting for Dean to let his guard down. And that hadn't taken long.

He and his brothers, along with members of the Marshal's Bluff police, had scoured the city, eventually finding the group of homeless who'd relocated without warning several days before. They'd gotten wind of trouble afoot after Mikey was attacked, and they'd wisely taken themselves out of the crosshairs.

Unfortunately they didn't have any information about Joseph Knolls.

Dean had been forced to call it a night when he'd dozed off for a moment behind the wheel and realized he was no longer useful to anyone. In that condition, he was a danger. So he'd gone home, where of course, he wasn't able to sleep.

He'd tossed and turned on his bed, the scent of her trapped in the fabric of his sheets and pillows. Images of her alone, terrified, injured or worse had pulled him awake each time his exhausted mind and body dared relax. He'd given up before dawn and made coffee.

Finn had called soon after and ordered him to the ranch for breakfast. The whole crew had been there when he'd arrived, and Mama was already cooking.

Mrs. Homes and Blakely were sleeping.

Dean's heart broke for the older woman and her grandchild upstairs. He couldn't imagine the pain of knowing both his children were missing, both in the hands of a killer.

"We tapped the landlines of Mrs. Tippin's siblings and Mr. Tippin's brother," Finn said, shoveling grits into his mouth by the fork load. "Mrs. Tippin called her sister. She used her cell phone, so we were able to get a location on the couple. State troopers are en route to collect and return them. They were halfway across the state at a resort spa. We brought the sister and her husband in for questioning last night."

Dean's gaze shot to his. "You're just telling me? What did they say?"

Finn placed a hand between them, palm side down, as if suggesting Dean relax. "We got them out of bed and brought them to the station in separate cruisers." He smiled. "It took all of five minutes for the husband to realize this was about his in-laws. He had no problem answering our questions. His wife was slower to cooperate, but it didn't matter. Her spouse had already told us the Tippins wanted to meet for lunch somewhere outside town and borrow cash. He'd said no, and that had caused a marital spat that lasted until they went to bed. He was still worked up about it when we spoke."

Austin set his fork on an empty plate and swigged his coffee. "They probably wanted cash so they could avoid making any bank withdrawals or using their credit cards. I'm guessing they never thought about the police tapping phone lines."

"We were lucky so many of their relatives still have landlines," Finn said.

Dean scrubbed both hands through his hair. "How long until the Tippins arrive?"

Finn checked his watch. "Any time now."

"Let's go." Dean grabbed his truck keys. "I want to talk to them."

Lincoln rose from the opposite end of the table, a warning in his small smile. "Hold up now. I don't think you should get anywhere near those folks."

"Why not?"

Lincoln's smile grew. "Oh, I don't know. Maybe because you'll say the wrong thing, threaten someone you shouldn't, or knock this Tippin guy into next week and get sued. Potentially lose your PI license."

Dean scowled, forcing his hands over his hips and willing himself not to lash out in his mama's kitchen. "Well, I'm not staying here, if that's what you're suggesting."

Finn wiped his mouth and stood, facing Dean. "How about you promise not to threaten or punch anyone, and I let you sit in the observation room and watch from behind the mirror while I talk to each of them?"

Dean glanced at Lincoln, then met Finn's gaze with a nod.

Austin carried his plate and cup to the sink, then kissed their mama's cheek. "I'm going with those two. Sounds like they're planning a party."

Lincoln made a *pft* sound and sat, returning to his meal. Apparently he wasn't interested in a trip to the police department. That was probably for the better. The last few times he'd been there, he was under arrest.

DEAN AND AUSTIN took seats inside the observation room and watched as Finn interviewed the Tippins. It didn't take long for Mr. Tippin to crack. His wife seemed genuinely confused about everything she was asked, and Dean got the feeling she was left out of quite a bit when it came to her husband's side hustle.

Tippin, on the other hand, started talking as soon as Finn dropped Joseph Knolls's name and said he'd traded information for a lesser sentence. Tippin turned red, then gave up everything he knew about the man who seemed to act as the crime ring's muscle.

According to Tippin, violence was forbidden, but Knolls couldn't seem to help himself. He called him an unhinged miscreant and gave Finn a number of ways to contact the man in question. Including the name of Knolls's girlfriend, whose home he occasionally shared.

The door beside Dean opened, and Finn entered the observation room with a manila file folder in hand. "Uniforms are picking up the girlfriend."

Austin clapped Dean on the shoulder. "Closer every minute."

Maybe so, but Nicole had been missing all night. Cari had been missing for days, and their abductor had less and less to lose by killing them.

Finn's phone buzzed. He checked the screen, brow furrowing. "The uniform picking up the girlfriend called dispatch. Apparently she and Knolls are on the outs and she's already talking. Knolls makes daily trips to a storage unit in Elizabeth City. She's been tracking his cell phone in case he was seeing another woman."

Dean pushed onto his feet with a jolt of fresh adrenaline. "Let's go."

NICOLE SLEPT AT her sister's side, waking at every small sound, afraid Cari would disappear. The small cut on Nicole's throat had scabbed. Now it itched and burned. The goose egg on her head continued to throb, but her head hurt slightly less, until she moved.

Her empty stomach moaned with discomfort, as did the muscles in her neck, back and shoulders.

Cari whimpered in her sleep.

According to her sister, someone had delivered a jug of water and flashlight a short while after Knolls left her at the storage unit. The door had rolled up far enough for the items to be inserted, then the door was closed. Nicole wasn't sure if that had been Tippin or his wife, but she didn't think for a second it had been Knolls. He was far too callous to care.

Anticipation bounced and buzzed in her system as she awaited his return. She and Cari had made a plan before falling asleep. Cari was too weak and sore to fight, but she was sure she could run. When the door opened today, they'd be ready.

Meanwhile there was still hope that Dean or Finn would find them first. Maybe it wouldn't come to that, and Cari wouldn't have to run. She hadn't eaten in days, and her water jug was empty. She was petite, but Nicole couldn't carry her, at least not very fast or far.

Facing off with a cold-blooded killer wasn't something either of them was up for, but an even more worrisome thought was that Knolls might simply never return. And no one would find them.

The low rumble of a car's engine straightened her spine.

Cari sat upright beside her.

They exchanged a look and put the plan into action. Cari turned her flashlight on and set it on the floor. Then they tiptoed silently toward the door and crouched behind a row of boxes, praying Knolls wouldn't spot them immediately.

The barrier rolled up with a thunderous racket.

The sky outside was fire. Bright flames of orange and red against a distant gray horizon.

Sunrise.

"All right," Knolls called, his voice low and rough. "Wake up. Your little friends crossed a line. They took my girl to the station. Now I'm going to send their girls to the emergency room. But y'all won't be surviving the experience." He skulked past the boxes where they hid, too tunnel-visioned to bother looking around. As expected, he headed straight for the light, attention fixed on the back of the unit. "No one messes with me like this. No. One."

Adrenaline coursed through Nicole's system as she gripped Cari's hand. And they ran.

Fresh air crashed over them in a tidal wave, and Nicole's lungs seemed to expand fully for the first time in hours, devouring the cool, sweet oxygen. The dewy air met her sweat-slicked skin, invigorating and pushing her ahead.

"We should take the car," Cari said as they ran past, ducking into the next row of units. "He might've left his keys in the ignition."

They'd had this talk last night, but Nicole had insisted they just run. They couldn't afford to waste time, and if he had the keys with him, those lost moments could ruin their escape. Every second was too precious; it wasn't worth the risk.

Cari had agreed, but as they dashed passed the parked car, she looked and sounded uncertain.

A Godzilla-worthy roar echoed through the morning air, peppered with cuss words and the sounds of bursting boxes. He'd realized Nicole and Cari were gone.

The ominous sound of a low chuckle that followed made Nicole's blood run cold.

Joseph Knolls knew they couldn't have gone far, and he was up for the game.

They'd unintentionally invited a predator on a manhunt.

Chapter Twenty-Three

Nicole and Cari ran down the next aisle of storage units, moving in the opposite direction the car had been facing, hoping to find a way out.

Cari panted beside her, struggling to keep up. Her bare feet slapped against the ground. The high heels she'd worn to the party had been left behind for practicality.

"I've got you," she whispered. She checked over her shoulder to see her sister nod as tears streamed over her cheeks. The pain in her expression was undeniable. Her battered frame was thoroughly covered in bruises and cuts, all visible in the daylight.

She'd hidden how badly she was hurting, and Nicole's heart ached at the sight of her, but they had to keep going.

"We can do this," she promised. "Just keep your feet moving, and we'll be okay. We can do anything together."

She scanned the space over Cari's shoulder, then turned forward once more, surprised their captor hadn't yet followed.

Was he still searching the unit for them? Had he given chase in the wrong direction?

The sound of a car's revving engine stopped Nicole in her tracks.

Cari doubled over, catching her breath.

Images of Darla's gruesome death returned like a freight train, and suddenly the road they traveled between storage units felt more like a rat's maze than an escape route. If Knolls came for them by car, there'd be nowhere to run.

Tires squealed, and Nicole's heart banged wildly against her ribs.

The Charger spun into view, smoke rising from its tires as they painted a patch of blackness across the asphalt. Then the car stopped suddenly, facing them head-on and separated by half the length of the long row of storage units.

Knolls torqued the engine, and the car's frame tilted with barely tamped power.

Cari screamed, and Nicole turned them back the way they'd come. "Run!"

DEAN WAS IN his truck and on the highway before Finn and his team could pull themselves together. The moment they had an address on the storage unit in question, he was out the door. Austin's truck was in his rearview, and Dean's chest tightened with pride and appreciation. He had no idea what he'd find when he reached his destination, maybe nothing, or maybe his worst nightmare. Either way, he was glad once again to be a Beaumont. Things could've gone differently for him and his only biological brother, Jake, but fate had delivered them into a family his childhood mind hadn't even known to ask for.

Austin was here, and he'd have Dean's back, whatever came. He was probably also the only thing capable of stopping Dean from ripping Knolls into pieces if the man was anywhere within reach when they arrived.

Sounds of a racing engine broke through the quiet morning air as Dean took the final turn toward his destination. A black Charger spun into view atop the nearby hill, braking to a rocking stop at the end of one set of storage units.

Dean raced up the incline toward the Charger with Austin on his tail.

The car waited, shifting in place with each rev of its engine.

Austin broke away, circling the units while Dean headed toward the Charger.

The car broke forward with a scream of tires, and Dean's heart plummeted.

At the end of the aisle, two fast-retreating figures were running for their lives.

NICOLE WRAPPED HER arm around her sister, slowing her pace to help Cari, as if they could escape the car. "Run!" she yelled again, as the Charger launched forward.

They were almost at the end of the row.

The distant sound of sirens teased her ears, but

even if help was on its way, it wouldn't arrive in time to save them.

Cari cried out as Nicole jerked her around the corner and against a roll-up door in the next row.

She couldn't keep running, so they needed another plan.

"Press your back against the wall," Nicole said, throwing an arm across her sister's middle to hold her in place. "When the car makes its turn, it won't be able to hit us here. It'll have to back up and reposition. We can run again when that happens."

Cari nodded, face red and eyes closed, narrow body trembling against the orange door.

As predicted, the Charger appeared in the space of a heartbeat, spinning at the end of the lane, but it didn't stop as Nicole had expected. Instead, it flew past, the sound of another engine on its heels, and the sirens growing louder.

"We're not alone," Nicole panted, relief filling her eyes with hot tears. "We're going to make it."

Dean's truck swung into view then barreled past, chasing Knolls and his amped-up car.

Nicole's hair fluttered in the wake of the vehicles.

Another roar broke Nicole's reverie, and she started at the sight of a pickup racing toward them from the opposite direction. The truck's driver waved frantically through the open window.

"Austin!"

She tugged Cari's arm, and her sister's body slumped forward, collapsing onto the ground.

The truck was beside them in a second, the door opening as she fell to her sister's side.

"I've got her," he called, closing the distance in a rush. "Get in."

Nicole obeyed, trusting him completely with their lives. She threw herself into the truck's cab, and he passed her sister onto her lap like a child before jumping behind the wheel once more.

They'd cleared the end of the aisle and made a turn toward the exit when the Charger reappeared.

The black car flew at them, seemingly determined to collide head-on in the space running along the end of all the rows.

"He's going to kill us," Nicole whispered, holding her sister more tightly and knowing it wouldn't be enough. Cari needed a safety belt they didn't have. And they all needed a miracle.

Austin smashed the brake pedal and jerked the shifter into Reverse, tossing Nicole and Cari forward then back in two sharp moves.

The Charger came faster, eating up the space as Austin piloted them away.

Nicole's heart wedged into her throat, attention fixed on their predator and unprepared to die.

A flash of black on black exploded before them in a teeth-rattling boom!

The Charger flew sideways, shattered glass bursting into the air as the car spun and bounced, end over end, on the asphalt before crashing to a stop against a telephone pole.

A smashed black truck was left in its wake. Front

end annihilated. Airbag fully deployed, blood splattered over the ballooned material.

Dean.

THE DAYS FOLLOWING Dean's collision were touch and go. Nicole moved into the hospital waiting room, much to the dismay of some hospital staff. A thorough exam of her head had confirmed she wasn't concussed, and after an IV of fluids, she'd been released for home. Dean and Cari hadn't been as lucky.

Cari had gone home the next day, after a night of observation and a long line of tests for internal injuries and broken bones. She'd been severely dehydrated and in desperate need of sustenance as well as fluids. The emergency room doctors had cleaned and bandaged her wounds, then admitted her. Their dad had finally responded to their mom's calls on the matter after Cari had already returned home.

Dean had gone straight to surgery.

Nicole set up accommodations in the waiting room beside Mrs. Beaumont and several seats continually occupied by the Beaumont brothers. Even Jake, an ATF officer and Dean's biological brother, had traveled from Memphis to be there.

By the time Dean moved from the ICU to a semi-private room a week later, it was fair to say a good chunk of the staff was glad to see him and his entourage moving on.

Now, just three weeks later, Dean was on the mend in big ways. The room was filled with balloons, flowers and enough food to feed the entire medical staff, plus a whole slew of loved ones. Per the usual.

"Everything's looking as it should," an older male doctor said, smiling warmly at Dean's chart. "You're healing at an incredible rate, no doubt thanks to this group." He tipped his head at the multitude of bodies around him. "Sometimes love really is the best medicine. Keep it up, and I think you'll be on your way home in the morning."

Nicole squeezed his hand, heart swelling and silent prayers rising. They'd all survived. They'd all healed. And soon, they'd all be home.

"Tomorrow," Dean repeated, deep blue eyes locked on hers.

Nicole raised the penny on her necklace into view. Emergency room doctors had found it in his pocket following the crash. A small heart shape had been punched through the coin, and she'd slid her favorite chain through it, keeping the talisman close to her heart while Dean healed. He'd carried her heart with him a long while, and she was ready to return the favor for as long as he'd allow. She rubbed the coin between her thumb and first finger, a habit she'd formed these last few weeks. "I can stay with him for the next few weeks while he heals," she told the doctor, "or at least until he's cleared to drive again."

"Lucky me," Dean said, lips curling into a playful smile.

The doctor gave some basic care and follow-up appointment information, then took his leave.

Cari moved to Nicole's side, Blakely dozing in her arms. The bruises from Cari's time in captivity had healed, but the emotional trauma would be there for a while. So she and Blakely were moving to Charleston with their mother and grandparents. She needed a soft place to land while she got the counseling and rest she needed.

Saying goodbye was something neither of them was prepared for, so they didn't mention her move more than absolutely necessary. And Nicole did her best not to think of how empty her apartment would seem without them.

Nicole rose from her chair to kiss Blakely's cheek and slide her arm around Cari's back. Cari's head tipped instantly to rest on Nicole's shoulder.

"So," Cari said. "What are you waiting for? I'm leaving soon, in case you haven't heard."

Nicole wrinkled her nose. Cari and their mother had just arrived. She craned her head for a look at her sister, but Cari was speaking to Dean.

"What am I always waiting on?" Dean asked. "Finn."

"Who's waiting on me?" Finn appeared in the doorway, dressed in a gray suit and blue tie.

"I am," Dean said. "It's about time."

Mrs. Beaumont waved a hand at Dean, then greeted Finn with a kiss on his cheek. "You look so handsome. Did you see any social workers at the courthouse today?"

Finn slid a sidelong look at his mama.

Nicole smiled. Cari laughed. Finn had been in love

with a social worker once. Everyone had loved her, and Nicole never did get the whole story on that, but she hoped they'd find their way back to each other one day, the way she and Dean had.

"Court went well," Finn said, changing the subject and clasping his hands. "Joseph Knolls will be going to jail on two counts of murder, Darla's and Dr. Maline's. Two counts of kidnapping, assault, blackmail, all of it. The Tippins are both getting jail time, though Mrs. Tippin will likely have the bulk of her sentence suspended. Her husband, however, will be spending a long chunk of his time behind bars. All their assets are being seized in conjunction with the blackmail scheme, so when they get out, they'll have a lot of rebuilding to do. All in all I'd say justice was served. How'd your morning exam go?" he asked Dean.

"I get out tomorrow."

Nicole's mom moved into view, her phone raised as if she might take a picture. "I have my folks on a video call," she said, turning her screen to pan the room.

Dean waved at the camera. "Hey, Mrs. and Mr. Dupree."

"Hello, Dean," her grandmother called.

"What?" her grandpa asked.

Nicole's mother turned the volume down and smiled. "Okay. All set. Go on."

Nicole frowned at the suddenly still room.

Even Lincoln, though perpetually silent, had moved to stand near the hospital bed with everyone else.

"Nicole," Dean said, drawing her eyes back to his.

Something in his tone sent goose bumps down her arms. "Yeah?"

"I planned to take you to our spot at the coast," he said. "I had a picnic in mind with something from each of our best dates. Photos from the county fair. Wine from that vineyard you love. Mama's apple pie."

Nicole returned to her seat, reaching for his hand. "We can still go."

Couldn't they?

Dean smiled. "I'd like to think there are hundreds of picnics in our future. Maybe fifty or sixty years' worth."

Nicole smiled.

Mrs. Beaumont pressed a tissue to the corner of each eye and latched onto her husband's arm.

Nurses gathered outside the doorway.

When Nicole's gaze slid back to Dean, he held a small ring box on his palm.

"Nicole Marie Homes," he said, tugging her closer to his side. "I've got something I've been meaning to ask you."

Shock stole her breath as she admired the thin gold band and glimmering solitaire.

"Will you accept this ring as a promise of my love?" he asked. "Will you wear it always, knowing it represents my heart in your hands?"

Tears of pride, honor and love raced over her cheeks. "Are you—" She faltered, checking the warm smiles all around her, then the tear-filled eyes of the man she loved. "Are you asking me—"

"I am begging you to be my wife," he said, humbled and smiling before her.

And Nicole said yes.

* * * * *

Look for more books in Julie Anne Lindsey's miniseries Beaumont Brothers Justice, when Always Watching *goes on sale next month. You'll find it wherever Harlequin Intrigue books are sold!*

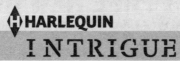

HARLEQUIN
PLUS

Try the best multimedia subscription service for romance readers like you!

Read, Watch and Play.

Experience the easiest way to get the romance content you crave.

Start your **FREE TRIAL** at
<u>www.harlequinplus.com/freetrial</u>.